I0762041

BURN IN HELL DARYL FLYNN

CONOR GALVIN

UNIVERSAL
BOOKS

Burn in Hell Daryl Flynn
First published in 2021 by Universal Books
360 North Circular Road, Phibsborough,
Dublin 7, Ireland D07 KX36
www.universalmedia.ie

ISBN 978 1 7399742 0 6
A CIP catalogue record for this book is available from the British Library.

September 2021
1 2 3 4 5 6 7 8 9 10

This book is set in Baskerville
Designed by Universal Media
Cover image adapted from
Stephen Bergin on Unsplash

Conor's style of writing exposes the sneering cynical Dublin veneer of living life at the hard edge of society. His brute force observations on the manic struggles of ordinary people behind closed doors will both captivate and challenge. *Burn in Hell Daryl Flynn* is his debut novel and only the start of a journey into the mundane, the macabre and the tormented undercurrent of Irish society.

As a graduate of Trinity College, Conor knows all about the perils which exist beyond the famous front arch. His assimilation into Trinity life saw him infiltrate the golden circles of the Campanile. This novel will lift the lid on the darker secrets of this conflicted institution as the chief protagonist is catapulted into Freshers week mayhem.

To the memory of Andrew Curtin
and all those who continue to fight their demons...

To the beautiful Mick & Annette Royce. You left us far too soon. You always said my time in Trinity would amount to something... not sure you had this in mind! Love always.

Flynn

Chapter One: No Way Out

Rachel sat pensively at her kitchen table. Her father shifted his weight from foot to foot, eager to get down to the Watermill for his evening serving of pints.

Terry Reilly, by all accounts a very promising footballer back in the day until ligament damage sabotaged that dream. Now he was a bus driver. He had taken a long time to come to terms with a life of mediocrity. Like many aspiring sports people, he had nothing to fall back on. His uncle found him a job driving the buses, and his evolution from superstar to ham-and-egger was complete. A long and arduous rut developed. Drive the buses then reconvene to the Watermill for four or five pints and talk about how the country is doomed, too many immigrants taking up jobs and how 'the Dubs would win fuck-all until they got a decent manager.' The Watermill self-help group were blanket underachievers. Those who had given up the ghost on life a long time ago and were content to be spectators rather than protagonists. Only two weeks of a holiday in Courtown, Wexford, punctured Terry Reilly's daily routine. The Watermill was a bastion of lost souls who would clock in at an exact hour every day as if compelled by the calling bell of Islam. Any change in routine was sacrilege. Terry was just another lost soul, too long-lost in the fields of misery to realise that there might be a way back. His universe became impenetrable. His lifestyle blinded him from tackling the real issue, the emotional turmoil of his daughter, now sitting hopelessly lost in front of him. It wasn't that he didn't love her, he loved Rachel very much, but Terry could never get the words out. He lacked the emotional skill set, and invariably his interactions would be reduced to "ye need to lose a few pounds, Love, and stop eating them fuckin' doughnuts." His wife Anne had badgered him about having a heart-to-heart with Rachel until finally, he relented, reluctantly.

On the fateful night in question, he was antsy. He couldn't see the point in sitting down to talk through emotional issues with his daughter. 'Lose a few pounds, get a bit of exercise, and she'll be fuckin' grand.' His attendance was tokenist at best. Deep down, he felt that the world owed him a favour. He was destined for greatness, and now look at him. What a favour life had given him, an obese daughter with mental health issues. All he could think about was exiting the claustrophobic kitchen and getting four minutes of oxygen in his lungs before arriving at the Watermill - rack up a few pints and sure everything would be grand.

Rachel was now the only child in the house. Her brother left for Australia to work on the buildings a few years previously. Her mother, Anne, was a soft character, a timid soul who never found a foothold in life. Terry walked all over her, the quintessential doormat. Her problem standing up for herself was not limited to her domestic situation. Her work life in Debenhams was poisoned by bullying. Instead of fighting fire with fire, she fought fire with acceptance. When she looked at Rachel, she saw an almost mirror image of herself. Tough love was missing. She became a facilitator for Rachel's depression and would even go shopping for junk food for her daughter upon request. On that fateful evening, she noticed an uplift in Rachel's mood as she sat by the table. Terry stood by the sink and after small talk and smiles from his daughter he decided there was no further dialogue required. "Sure your Ma has me standing here like a fuckin' eejit, you're bleedin' grand, Love." Less than ten minutes into their supposed intervention, he was gone. He touched her right cheek with the palm of his right hand. A touch from a calloused hand, but gentle nonetheless. Rachel could feel a certain warmth, albeit cloaked in reticence. He ambled past her to grab his coat and headed for the liberation of the stress-free plains of the Watermill. That would be the last time he would see his daughter alive again.

Rachel became entranced in a moment of reflection. She stared intensely at her mug. It had been one of her favourite pieces of delph, a reminder of her past life. The faded imprint of Boyzone looked back at her. She still had posters in her room, attesting to her fanaticism. A time when she had something to cling on to. The carefree days before the demons intoxicated her fragile soul. She took a long draught of her sugary tea until only a quarter remained. The last quarter was the most delicious. Save the best for last. The flawless deposition of the escaping sugar particles as they gathered in one last heroic stance at the bottom of the teacup. She brought the mug to her lips. The first few sugar particles climbed over her bottom lip, she realised that she would never experience this sensation again. The last supper. But the conversation continued, just Rachel and her mum, Anne. After a short conversation of false promises, Rachel knew just what to say: "to be honest I'm starting to feel a bit better about things,"-a perfectly rehearsed response to extricate herself from the awkwardness.

Anne wanted the best for her daughter, but knew that she didn't have the answers she needed. Her soft centre forced her to live more in hope than conviction. "The only thing I want is to see you happy again, Love." Her eyes welled up as she leaned in to embrace her daughter. She attempted to wrap her arms around the full perimeter of Rachel's frame, but the sheer girth of flesh meant she only hugged three quarters of her. Anne closed her eyes as she held her in a long, warm embrace, not knowing this would be for the last time. All the years of nurture from the womb. All the years of love were ending in this epilogue.

After several seconds, Rachel recoiled and looked her Mam in the eyes, "I will be happy, Mam, I'll be happy very soon, I promise." Rachel retreated to her room. From the drawer in her desk she took out an A4 notepad and pen, her favourite pen, a pink troll pen with fluffy hair. She penned the following:

'Dear World,

There is only one way to end this hurt. This world is not for me any more. Consider this the end of my suffering as opposed to the end of my life. I blame nobody else for my demise. I carry only good memories into the next life - wherever that may be.

See you all on the other side,
Rachel'

She had rehearsed those words hundreds of times in her head, so it was a simple rehash. She read it back one last time for spelling mistakes before folding it and putting it in her pocket. She smiled at the irony of it all, checking her own suicide note for spelling mistakes. Rachel told her mum she was going for a walk to get some air and quietly slipped out of the house for the last time.

She wore the simple attire of a tracksuit, hoodie and runners. She smiled at herself in the hall mirror, knowing that soon it would all be over, the end of her pain which had haunted her all her life. She would never have to look at her own face again. A feeling of empowerment came over her as she finally felt in control. Pretty soon, Rachel Reilly would be no more. This world could no longer drag her into the depths of hell.

The walk through St. Annes Park was a retracing of a path she had taken many times with Flynn. There was a full moon and a beautiful tranquillity about the park. Each step was a step closer to freedom. Only three hundred yards left. The wooden tripod across from the playground which supported the zip line. Twenty more yards left. Rachel didn't break stride. Her mind was in a different stratosphere, removed from the hurt and trauma this would cause if she didn't rethink her actions. All that remained were three wooden steps to the top of the platform. She negotiated these with ease, unburdened by second thoughts. Without pausing for any further reflection, she stood at the top of the platform and affixed the cable cord around her neck. One last breath and one last look up at the moon and stars. Rachel stepped off the platform. The initial jolt violently shattering her wind pipe, her body involuntarily tried to gasp for breath before darkness descended for the last time. The moon and stars shone brightly above her lifeless body.

Flynn

Chapter Two: Wrong Side of the Tracks

A ghost stared back at Daryl Flynn from his bedroom mirror. Occasionally he wondered if he was alive at all. Perhaps this was purgatory after death. A soulless wasteland. A punishment from God. A permanent vacuum resided in his gut. Another day of going through the motions, gripping the shadows. He closed his eyes at night, indifferent of whether he would regain consciousness in the morning. He ran his fingers down the sides of his face, as if looking to claw off an illusionary mask. Anything to vanquish the ghost of Daryl Flynn.

He squirted a large dollop of hair gel onto the palm of his hand and rotated his hands in an anti-clockwise direction. He spread his fingers and applied the perfectly dispersed contents around his hair, moulding his jet-black hair into a 'curtains' hold. His unblinking sea-blue eyes stared back at him, he felt disturbed when he held his own gaze. It was as if his empty soul was upon view. His pale complexion was crowned with a square jaw and a veneer of thin black stubble. He washed his face and dried himself off with the hand towel. Pausing for another long, lingering, self-loathing look at himself in the mirror, *'Well Flynn, I'm sure they'll fuckin' love ye in the Trin! No doubt you'll fit right in.'* His eyes narrowed, *'Ye better shape up, ye useless fuck.'*

Bare chested and naked apart from his blue and navy jocks, his large frame was an imposing presence in the mirror. Large in physical stature yet reduced to a pygmy within. *'I wonder how many other Trinity students woke up in council houses this morning?'* he quietly theorised. *'On the bright side at least*

Flynn

I won't be meeting any degenerates from St. Davids in there, none of those Neanderthals would be let within an arse's roar of the place, be grateful for small mercies Flynn.' Flynn gazed at the Trinity prospectus on his bed, the front featured a picture of the famous campanile tower. The crest, the lion, the harp, the book and castle neatly emblazoned. Everything about it smacked of elitism. He had read some brief history on the place, albeit an Irish account. It was founded by Queen Elizabeth I in 1592 and for centuries afterwards was controlled by the great and the good of Protestant society. Its educational fortitude had even survived the Irish famine in 1847 as the well-fed elite were educated whilst the mouths of the peasants turned green with hunger. Archbishop McQuaid even banned Catholics from attending, a ban which endured till 1970. *'Maybe he didn't want Catholics attending, as he couldn't violate them on Protestant territory.'*

His body shook as flashbacks of his ordeal came shooting back, piercing his gut and ripping through his cranium. His body broke into violent perspiration and jolted as he heard those poisonous noises inside his head. That grotesque snarling and laboured breathing. The violation. He felt like screaming out and putting his fist through the wall, but then things subsided. The moment passed and his body temperature regulated. *'Dirty rapist bastards, fuck the Catholic Church.'* They had damaged him, but the truth is he was damaged long before then. He took a deep breath, He pulled on a pair of blue jeans and slipped a white t-shirt over his head. He couldn't bear the feel of even his own flesh when the flashbacks started. An internal annexation. *'Bad enough waking up in this shithole without the mental torture as well.'* He walked back over and looked in the mirror. *'It can't go on like this.'*

Flynn

His social anxiety was crippling. And here he was, getting changed in a council house in Artane to cross the Liffey to mix it with the entitled class of private schools and wealth. *'You're a fuckin' nobody, Flynn.'* A psychotic looking Uma Thurman stared back at him from a giant poster on the wall. Her eyes were both seductive and violent. She held a smoking cigarette in her right hand as a gun lay upon the pillow in front of her. Her cleavage was moderately exposed as she lay forward wearing a black body top, blue jeans and black high heels. The poster advert of his favourite Quentin Tarantino film and regular source of masturbation.

He shunted into his white converse and drifted down the hall and into the kitchen. His mother stood at the sink looking shook as she rattled a few dishes around the draining board. Her tan line and stale perfume exposed the fact that she was out the night before. The sight of her first thing in the morning flooded his thoughts with more resentment. *'God knows where she was last night and with who?'* At this stage, Flynn didn't care. She turned sheepishly towards him, "eh… good morning, Daryl, do ye want anything?" She was evasive - a further giveaway of her antics and futile effort at a cover-up. She gazed out the kitchen window and into the back garden, incapable of eye contact. Such interactions had become commonplace. The soul had drained out of their relationship. "Nah, grand, heading off now," was his only retort. He had long ago stopped calling her "Ma" or "Mam" or "Mum" or referring to her in any kind of maternal way. Like many things in life, Flynn's thoughts on women embarrassed him. It ranged from hatred to confusion to almost physical violence.

Flynn

His Dad passed away when he was five. The typical photos and memories of a broken family to bereavement remain. The photo of himself and his Dad with an ice cream in Howth on a sunny day. Like a lot of childhood memories, when you think so much about a photo, the brain seems to create a one that was never there. He finds himself making memories that probably never existed. He never felt that loss. Five years on this planet yet he never remembers much of his Dad. His Dad's sister, Aunty Jean, spoke of nothing else except his Dad around him, over and over again. Like some post-traumatic stress victim rehashing the same hurt. Almost reaching out to him as if he needed more hurt. His Dad was dead, and he had few recollections of his own. They say they never speak ill of the dead, but his Dad was a troubled character. He burned through several jobs and was always in debt, trying to swim ahead of the shark. Died of an aneurysm they say, no life assurance, left the family almost destitute.

His sister Vanessa had been developing mental issues since her early teens, but they seemed to brush everything under the carpet. Deny everything and it will go away. She had finally been diagnosed with bipolar disorder, but only after an event which will haunt him forever. The night he heard his mother's screams. The night those screams came from his sister's room. He ran in to find her self-harming with a knife as his mother frantically failed to restrain her.

There were four years between them, at the time she was seventeen, and he was thirteen. His first feel of the female naked body was coated with blood.

Flynn

The unnatural grapple with your own sibling's naked body. Wrestling a blade away from her. His tears, his mother's frantic screams. It may have lasted ten minutes. Memories would come back like a steam train. More vivid, violent flashbacks of a different kind. Flynn wanted to smash his head off a wall, concussion might be the answer, but action wasn't his thing. Like a boat slowly taking in water far away from shore, he was trapped. Each day he felt himself being further submerged beneath the waves, slowly drowning. He never discussed with his sister the root cause of her upset or mental degeneration. He was too afraid.

Perhaps it was akin to what happened to him, or perhaps something even more harrowing. His own dark secret could remain buried deep in his soul until they shovelled soil over him in the boneyard. He knew deep down he was damaged.

Flynn's mother was the eldest of five children, she had been a talented Irish dancer back in the day and the sitting room cabinet was still filled with tacky trophies. She had gone to college and got a basic diploma, but never really furthered herself in her career after she met Flynn's father. No doubt she would have dreamed big back in her youth, but now she was widowed and living in a working-class estate in Artane with two fucked-up kids.

Flynn never felt sorry for her. He never felt sorry for anyone, all sympathy was reserved for himself. Sometimes after a few gins she would get emotional. It always took a few gins before she would try to engage him emotionally. She would then pour her heart out. Telling Flynn she was "lonely, hurt and miserable." She would tell him she loved him and was doing her best for a better life. He would simply look through her with disdain. *'Why the fuck did this woman put me on this planet?'* He would retreat to his room and close the door. She would often follow him and talk through the door before eventually giving up. She would go back to the kitchen sobbing, comforted by another half bottle of Gin before bed. A simple hug or show of love would have meant the world to her, but Flynn didn't have it in him, he was content to torture her further.

Every other minute spent in the house was barely functional. Conversation was non-existent and limited to small talk.
- "How was school?"
- "Grand."

Anything further would result in doors banging. They all eventually just gave up on each other and resentment set in. His mother never made the house a home. It was always fragmented. Her moods would drift depending on the boyfriends she kept. Most of whom would disappear when seeing the potential baggage. I'm sure they told her what she wanted to hear. Told her that they would be her "life partner," that they would be there for her. Made her dream of better things. The long lunch dates and nights out. She wanted to introduce someone, but it never materialised. She was picked up one day by some fella called 'Frank' as Flynn happened to be coming home. It was awkwardness upon awkwardness. He looked at Flynn's mother with the same respect that Flynn would look at Rachel. A means to an end. His end. With his mother. It made Flynn sick.

Like the rest of them, he would disappear in a cloud of empty promises once he got his fill. Flynn had no idea if his mother was overly promiscuous or simply desperate, but at this stage he didn't care. She was just a further reminder of his misery, his crippling nerves, his low self-esteem and his lack of belonging. He daydreamed of killing Frank, he would make sure he tortured every sinew of this body before finally slitting his throat. He felt nothing as he theorised the manner of the killing, there was no heightened blood pressure or rapid heart beat. This actually worried Flynn. He wasn't a killer but something had to give. His anger at the world had to spill over eventually.

Flynn

Chapter Three: Science Girl

Flynn had convinced himself that today would be different. Positive self-talk on the bus, *'Come on now Flynn, you loser-fuck, today is the day we leave the past behind.'* He bounded up Dame Street with a spring in his step, a rarefied mental state of confidence. He almost felt good about himself. College Green was fast approaching. The famous Front Arch was sucking him in like a vortex but suddenly each step triggered landmines of anxiety. He tried to fight it. 'Ah, please no, not today,' but the demons were alive within. Students filed past him in giddiness and expectation. Full of hope. Flynn slunk against the outside railings. He turned back towards Westmoreland street and thought about running. His eyes began to water as he reflected on his pathetic state. *'Why me? Why the fuck do I feel like this?'*

Once again, what should have been a happy occasion is being sabotaged by his demons. The feeling of inadequacy engulfed his spirit. *'False confidence evaporates when you hate the person within.'* The past was repeating itself – paralysis by anxiety. *'Wrong school, wrong look, wrong family, wrong fuckin' everything'* he reminds himself. All the negatives smash into his brain like a tsunami. He can no longer stand his full height and folds over a like a cheap suit. He curses the place he's from and wishes to be like someone else, anybody else. A violent sweat pierces his brow as he contemplates self-destruction and one day ending it all. He reminds himself that he wouldn't have the guts. He could never pull a trigger, knife his wrists or hang himself from a rope. Far away in his unconscious fantasy he's getting a Las Vegas introduction to Front Square, *'And now, Ladies and Gentlemen, introducing… The mass gathering applauded the arrival of the Alpha. His male peers give way out of respect as the girls shoot him lustful glances.'* In reality, nobody takes any notice of Flynn as he hugs the outside railings, unable to control his palpitating heart. All the years of ghosting through life for once serves him well as nobody casts him a second glance.

He swallows deeply and shunts himself forward. He goes from darkness to light and finally feels the famous cobble lock beneath his feet. It's Freshers Week and there are stands everywhere, a giant gauntlet runs through to Front Square. It's manic. Throngs of fresher students bustle past, whooping and hollering. Flynn visualises a giant sinkhole opening up, anything to put himself out of his misery. *'This was a fuckin' mistake.'* He looks around in a daze. A fine chiselled fella dons a Trinity hoodie and talks to a beautiful-looking girl, she's upper-class Southside and hangs on his every word. She's from money and private school education. A galaxy away from some fat yoke that Flynn would pull at the local disco after a flagon of cider had nullified his nerves. Prey on the weak, the wounded gazelles. Targeting anything higher on the food chain would result in rejection. Flynn is awestruck by the ease at which "Trinity hoodie man" engages the beauty queen. A mixture of jealously and a reinforcement of his inadequacy sweeps over him. The drowning begins.

Flynn's first encounter is with a girl wearing an oversized Science Club t-shirt. The girl has brown curly hair and freckles galore, but seems content enough in herself. Too content. That vital sense of belonging, even to a shower of freaks. Strength in numbers. She obviously found her niche in the Science Club. The t-shirt hangs over a pair of ragged blue jeans which flows like the tributary of a river into a pair of black and white Adidas runners. So content in herself that she hasn't bothered with a layer of make-up. *'What the fuck is she so smug about?'* he barks to himself. She tries to look into Flynn's eyes but he shuns eye contact.

A show of weakness. No litmus test from the laboratory required. Flynn tries to maintain composure, but his false blasé demeanour is starting to go up in flames. Like a skunk, he's stinking the place out. The rotten stench of low self-esteem.

"Hey there! Would you like to join the Science Club? Free drinks today in the Buttery this afternoon from four!" She addresses him in the clinical, carefree manner that pilots address nervous passengers during heavy turbulence. She knows something he doesn't. Flynn feels his chest tighten, palpitations trigger a further breathlessness. His mouth is dry. His first attempt to speak is stalled because the nerves have blocked the saliva reaching his throat. The tightening in the chest means he can't get the air from his lungs to formulate a word. The reddening of his face adds further humiliation. He has been laid bare and exposed by the first girl talking in this direction. "Trinity hoodie man" would just ignore her and better again "science girl" wouldn't even approach "Trinity hoodie man" as she would be told to 'Fuck off', or sling her hook or plainly just be blanked. *'Why can't I be more like "Trinity hoodie man"'* seethes Flynn to himself. But he's drowning and she knows it. He's being torched. "Eh… No… I'm grand." The sentence hardly audible because it's aimed at the ground where Flynn wishes he's buried. She looks at him in a manner of confused impatience that she may have wasted three seconds of her time on this deadbeat.

Flynn

"Are you sure… free drinks in the Buttery?" Her voice trails off in a dismissive tone. As if she's talking to some complete moron who fails to grasp the significance of free drinks for students. This in itself is a measure of social rejection, being targeted by some weird curly haired girl from the Science Club. Flynn couldn't get the words out, strangled by nerves and paralysis, he gestured to say something but could only muster a half-hearted muttering. Mid-stutter she simply turns away, recognising that Flynn is simply an irrelevance, not just to the Science Club but to everyone. It wasn't the first time he had been dismissed but the demons inside him were burning like an inferno. The colour of humiliation illuminated his face. That unmistakable complexion of someone who is drowning with nerves, that doesn't belong in their environment. Standing there emotionally naked, a laughingstock, awkward, zero confidence, bitter, angry, but most of all hurt. There was love for Flynn in the world, but he couldn't carry it with him, this feeling of inadequacy raged in his heart and overwhelmed his every action.

The cobble lock suddenly felt like it was moving under his feet, vertigo set in, unbalanced by anxiety and racked with nerves. He edged forward, not as a sign of defiance but simply because he was being jostled from behind, the tide of fresher students pushing him towards the front square. Turning back would mean facing back into the crowd, risking more people seeing his anxiety stricken face, they'd know this deadbeat was running back to the hole he crawled out from. He shuffled forwards and eyed up the open space of the front square in the distance. A perceived oasis in the desert. Room to breathe. Not exactly a prairie of freedom but at least more scope to be anonymous. Where he was now was simply claustrophobic, the thoughts of making eye contact, failing again and worst of all being judged. The judgement was not new, more reaffirming his own dark thoughts that he was *'a worthless piece of shit'*.

Observing those around him socialising freely was like drinking acid. It reminded him of how dysfunctional he really was and heightened his sense of bitterness. He felt an extraordinary longing for someone to just reach out and say "Flynner ye Legend, what's happening buddy?" Belonging. If that shout came he could stroll across to that person, sling down this bag, kick his feet up on a society table, start shooting the breeze and cracking jokes about the good-looking girls passing by. Instead, he was stuck in the sinking sand of loneliness, each passing second lessened his sense of self-worth. *'What the fuck is wrong with me? Fuck you, Daryl Flynn! Fuck you!'*

Flynn

Chapter Four: The Legend, The Loser and The Jesuits

Flynn looked down the gauntlet of stands. He was now three paces ahead of "science girl" who was now in conversation with one of her own and laughing hysterically. Her conversation with Flynn quickly forgotten. Not for Flynn. He remembered every interaction. Call it irrational hatred, call it what you want, but Flynn had a memory bank as long as the Suez Canal. The flames of hatred that would burn so brightly in his world but never dissipate. His first interaction on Trinity soil was a girl simply asking him if he wanted to join the science club with the addendum of a free piss up. Any other Fresher would acquit themselves with a simple yes or no, but not Flynn. Anyone who exposed his inner demons became an enemy. *'Why didn't she leave him the fuck alone, did he really look like someone who would join the fuckin' science club?'* She created a trigger inside him. Hand him a flyer and *'fuck off'* but, *'that bitch had stayed too long.'* A seed of revenge lodged within. He passed by the next few stands without much fuss, mainly apathetic students handing out flyers worn down by either hangovers or boredom. He was still unsteady on the cobble lock beneath his feet. He was rattled. One punch away from a knock-out.

He approached the hockey club stand which was manned by a posse of about a dozen lads and ladies all decked out in university team gear and flirting wildly amongst themselves. No doubt telling stories of past glories or comparing daddy's wealth. It occurred to him that a couple of lads at the table looked a bit older, obviously third or fourth years and therefore royalty in the land of the "freshers" - laugh at their jokes even if they weren't funny type of shite. Hockey was always a sport he wanted to try.

Flynn

He used to love hurling at underage levels but like life itself it just passed him by. He'd already made his mind up that this is one of the clubs he'd like to join. Just as he edged towards the table he felt a surge from behind and then a shout, "Hey you Guuuuuuuuys!" He gets bustled out-of-the-way by a red-headed teen wearing a Three Rock Rovers windbreaker, a pair of non-slip sailor shoes and baggy beige cords. At least six of the lads around the hockey table roar in unison, "Marloooowe! Marloooowe! Marloooowe!" Obviously, this is one "fresher" who won't have to break down any boundaries. Flynn was now standing alongside 'the great Marlowe' which made him completely invisible to the gathering. Royalty. The warm embrace of being on the inside. He grabbed the clipboard and demanded a pen from a stout looking girl with an English accent as he signed the registration sheet. 'Ross Marlowe.' No money seemed to change hands. Flynn waited pensively as Marlowe drifted to the back of the table to give hugs and high-fives to his fan club. Flynn now faced the jury all alone. There was no rush for his signature. One well-built lad with a gelled-up quiff eyed him up and asked "have you played before mate?" Flynn didn't make eye contact but managed to get out the words "Nah, a bit of hurling… would like to learn if that's alright?" Still no eye contact, maybe that was the secret. "Gelled-up-quiff man" chuckled, "Good man! Well, there's a fourths team that just love getting pissed, even if you're shit ye can still play for them." Flynn knew he was looking at him, but didn't return eye contact. "Thanks" he said as he handed £5 and the clipboard back to him. "Gelled-up-quiff man" took the clipboard and stuttered before saying "Em… there's a few initiations and club drinks tomorrow in the Pav Bar from seven bells if ye fancy?" This drew daggers from the fellow hockey fraternity at the table, this drinks bash was the preserve of the cool kids and the entitled, not an open invite and certainly not for some 'yellow-pack' rookie blow-in like Flynn. "Thanks" repeated Flynn, now looking down at the cobble lock as he shifted away and edged further down the gauntlet to the front square. The hockey club would sign up 412 members that day, but none more complex, volatile and unpredictable as Flynn.

"Gelled-up-quiff man" wasn't making friends, but at least had the good grace not to ridicule Flynn. Maybe deep down he knew Flynn was a lame duck and just threw him a lifeline. He could have drawn the rest of the posse in and repeated "hurling" out loud and taken him to the cleaners. But he didn't. His name was Andrew Magnier, a genuinely decent guy. He was from big money without the sense of entitlement. He wasn't oblivious to the plight of Flynn, he knew Flynn was vulnerable, but Magnier's outlook wasn't based on status. He was a Clongowes boy and Clongowes College carried a certain rite of passage on the hallowed turf of Trinity College.

Many of Clongowes College were the money men, the big backers for the university, the alumni who still wore the Trinity club ties and attended dinners drunkenly reminiscing on their glory days. They often say success breeds success and when daddy went to 'the Trin' and daddy's daddy went to 'the Trin', the bloodline all points to an exclusive club for the privileged. It becomes even more entrenched when daddy captained 'the Trin' hockey and is already in folklore. Look back through the records and all the wooden plaques in the Pav Bar showcasing the names of the club captains and presidents, and it's easy to see a recurring theme. The same surnames punctuate the roll of honour, serving as a reminder of the prerequisite of pedigree. Golden circles clubs were a major feature in Trinity, the trusted inner circle, the preservation of the family names and the desire for contingency of the status quo. It's often said the Jesuits endeavour is to instil humility in their students through their educational methods, and Magnier embodied this.

Life thus far had taught him to take people at face value. It was just what he felt deep inside, he always felt true to himself regardless of his second name. He grew up in a successful family, his father and uncles were extravagantly wealthy and most family interactions permeated a feeling of superiority and expectancy. It was in the bloodline. But it was also suffocating. The Jesuit education was in many ways the personification of one of the great dichotomies of life, bastions of education preaching humility yet only available to the wealthy fee-paying classes. Andrew Magnier saw it for what it was, yes he was privileged but he would never allow himself to feel and act entitled. The same couldn't be said for all his Clongowes comrades or the other factions of private school "freshers" who already hunted in packs around campus. They didn't need to reach out as they already had the comfort blanket of their crested brethren. Either way his interaction with Flynn, albeit brief, had given Flynn a lifeline, that simple conversation - a non-judgmental interaction which was a million miles away from the world Flynn had come from.

Back in St. David's, there was no such thing as giving a sucker an even break. Bully or be bullied. Fast fists or fast wits. A shortfall in either and your life was heading for misery. If you were being bullied, the best outcome was to become a ghost, someone who could walk through walls without being noticed. Flynn was lucky, the bullies never got up a head of steam when it came to him. Despite drowning in nerves and anxiety, he was clever and strategic underneath. He would have a sixth sense for who had it in for him and had the ability to become invisible. This was a survival reflex, not based on success but merely survival. Teenage years languishing in a dog-eat-dog Christian brother school was never a place he was going to shine. It was damage limitation. Survival was also dependent on a great deal of luck. Like the day Reilo decided he was going to give him a hiding for knocking him off his bike. Reilo was a big bastard and was on the top tier of the food chain which consisted of the tough men, travellers and psychopaths.

Reilo was always bombing around like a lunatic on his mountain bike. He never cared who he smashed into and if ye didn't like it, Reilo would smash your face in. Inadvertently one day he caught the strap on Flynn's backpack and ploughed into a tree on the school drive. Flynn stood frozen in shock as Reilo peeled himself off the ground and prepared for a violent assault. As he rolled up his sleeves and advanced towards Flynn the school bell rang and the yard teachers appeared. Reilo promised to "bate the bollix" out of him after school.

The school hours flew by that day. Flynn sat like a man in a holding cell about to be brought to the electric chair. He retained not a single word of any class that day. His body was paralysed by fear and violent anxiety. The overwhelming thoughts of getting beaten unconscious by this animal in front of everyone. He had tasted blood before. That unmistakable thick claret rolling from his nose into his mouth as a result of a smack of a stray hurley during yard. The difference then was he could get patched up without fear of further assault. Some people are built for combat, they almost become dehumanised by pain and blood to fight even harder, and then there are others, like Flynn, who fall by the wayside at the mere thought of physical conflict.

The seconds were ticking down to the bell ring and Flynn could almost feel himself dry retching. The adrenaline of preparing for a beating began draining his blood into the inner capillaries, rendering him in a state of almost paralysis. Word had got around and the vultures were circling. The expectant mob loving nothing better than a public slaying in the Colosseum. As the bell rang he began to pack away his books in ultra-slow motion. So slow in fact that the class was emptying out. The thought struck him that if he kept up this slow rate of packing up, he might see it through to the late evening. But then he would be a sitting duck outside the school gate and if not then, tomorrow morning and on and on it would go. There was no way out. He touched his face as if to feel his bone structure still intact. Damage limitation.

The figure of Charlie O'Shea loomed over him. "Do ye want me to hold your jacket while ye take your beating?" he asks. "Eh… nah thanks, I'm grand," said Flynn. Perhaps it may act as a shield, Flynn thought to himself. Reilo was an animal. This wasn't about revenge but more an excuse for him to dish out a proper beating. Flynn entered the yard and skirted round the edges of the green. He could make out the figure of Reilo coming towards him. It was November and the sun was sinking, he could gauge how far away the first punch was by the darkening shadow approaching. "You're fuckin'g dead now," said his assailant. Flynn's heightened senses allowed him to hear Reilo taking a breath as he drew back the first punch. Flynn didn't face him, instead looking at a spot on the ground, an almost perfect circle of chewing gum which had been worn into the ground over the years. He had learnt from his traumatic violations of the past that he could stare at the one spot, fixate his gaze and take the pain. Years previously it was a speckle of blood. Today it was chewing gum.

The punch caught Flynn solid on the side of the head. There was an extra loud CRACK upon impact. Flynn wondered had his skull just caved in but he could still see the chewing gum clearly and therefore realised he must still be conscious. Instead, it was Reilo who cried out in pain. His right fist had landed flush but what he failed to realise was the earlier fall had already fractured two metacarpals in his hand. The force of the second impact now led to the compound fracture of his hand and wrist.

The blood drained from Reilo's face as he surveyed the fresh bone no longer buried beneath his skin. The sickening CRACK originally drew 'oohs and aahs' from the onlookers before Reilo coiled away in anguish. Those present then saw the inhuman sight of fresh bone protruding out of Reilo's wrist like an oil rig from the sea. Everyone saw the contortion of the wrist apart from Flynn who was still focused on the chewing gum on the ground. He was still braced for the next onslaught. The pain and shock began to shoot through Reilo's nerve endings, his face became ghostlike and he began to hyperventilate. Flynn's code red body alert didn't allow him to break from his stoop and he remained still with a trance-like gaze at the gum. Pride still forced Reilo to get off two more kicks to Flynn's right hip area before slowly retreating backwards. As the pain overcame the adrenaline, Reilo momentarily fainted to the ground before regaining consciousness a few seconds later. His left hand held his mutilated right wrist up in the air like an Olympic torch. His face a maelstrom of panic, exasperation and pain. "Get fuckin' help, get fuckin' help," he uttered as he lay back on the ground. Flynn was still frozen in time. Dan Byrne came over to him and simply said, "ye should probably fuckin' scarper bud." Flynn edged away from the scene. There would be an ambulance arriving in St. David's, but it would be Reilo in the back and not him. A lot of survival depends on luck.

The capillaries recommenced blood flow back to the outside of Flynn's muscles and he could move again. Still expecting a sudden attack, he snailed his way towards the school gate. The capillaries started slowly pumping blood to his outer muscles. So much for the 'fight or flight' hormone meant to be in the human body. Flynn wondered if he had either as he ventured forth like an old, brittle woman walking the rose gardens of a nursing home. All the while he had fellow students whizzing past him and clapping him on the back. As if somehow he was the victor. "G'wan the Flynn!" said Murph as he cycled past. Murph was a traveller and always in trouble. Flynn could never remember any words ever being exchanged between them, let alone how he even knew his name. Perhaps under traveller law there was a preservation of honour for someone with a hard head. Murph lived on a halting site down in Clongriffin. Always seemed impenetrable to everything around him. Despite living in a caravan, Murph was not the sort to cower to anybody. Perhaps some mix of Wolverine blood coursing through his veins.

With each passing step Flynn began to thaw out and his pace slightly quickened. The November sun was now setting behind a mountain of clouds, Artane felt like a grey and soulless place. As he turned down the hill and headed for home he saw the lights of the ambulance coming towards him. Mixed emotions. Perhaps if he was in the back of that ambulance he would get a stint in hospital. Perhaps, if not for a compound fracture, Reilo would have kept pounding his skull until he left this world entirely. Flynn allowed himself to think about all the things in his life he wouldn't miss. As much as he hated himself and his environment Flynn had never contemplated suicide. He saw this life as some sort of purgatory, his quest was to escape from himself, not to kill himself.

Home offered no refuge from the demons of unhappiness. The thought did cross his mind of his mother and sister receiving the news of his demise. Would they be heartbroken and sad or would it be an extension of the misery they lived in? Thoughts drifted to his sister's mental illness, her self-harming and recent rut of depression. His mother now numbed by the struggle of life. Flynn didn't think about leaving them behind or the hurt that would cause. Was he a victim himself, or just plain selfish for something better? He would go home and close the door behind him and feel that lack of belonging, that lack of love, that sense of heightened insecurity. It takes a while to break that hope inside someone. That feeling that nothing good was ever going to happen and the reality that nothing good ever would. Flynn, however, still held out an intangible belief that he could get out of this environment and be different. Maybe not for the better, but just fuckin' different. Somewhere else where he would feel different, perhaps equally miserable but different.

At least college was an escape. The Leaving Cert was a memory exam, plain and simple. Read and regurgitate and hope for the best. One thing he had was a very good memory, quite extraordinary in fact. It was one of the reasons why he was so miserable. He couldn't forget the past. Perhaps his agent provocateur could also be his way out. Close by and on the Northside of the city was DCU and some other Institutes of Technology, though, he wanted another planet. Trinity College always seemed like another planet. Pickled in British history, jam-packed with international students, and most of all nobody from St. David's or anybody who knew him.

Flynn's house had a front door which was almost never used. There was a side lane which adjoined the back door and kitchen, which acted as the entrance. Even the post box was through the gate and hung on the wall beside the back door. The grass in the front garden was overgrown and encroaching shrubbery blocked any pathway to the front door, even if someone was well intended. Flynn heard his Aunty, Irene, remark that the last callers of that door were the Gardaí who called to inform his mother that his Dad would never come home again. Even back then the door frame was stiff from the lack of use. His mother had opened it and collapsed to the ground. It was the day the family's fortunes were sucked into an interminable pool of misery. For all the faults and volatility of his father he was still an anchor in the family unit, not someone to bring stability but at least the head count was four. Two lads and two ladies. Perfect dysfunctionality. After his passing the dynamic just became imbalanced. There was private grief but more bitterness. His Dad was selfish. No doubt he had his own demons. Don't speak ill of the dead and all that. After his initial passing the family comforted themselves in the rhetoric that he loved them all deeply, a hope fabricated by post-traumatic stress. Amazing how the sight of someone's coffin being lowered into the ground could somehow erase so many faults. However, over time, the empathy towards him drifted towards bitterness when Flynn's own demons surfaced. Blame it on genetics or lack of fatherly love and attention but the rhetoric of his Dad being a great family man soon died.

Every evening his homecoming followed the same routine and this evening was no different. He slumped down the lane and pushed open the side gate. There was that gentle reverberation and sound like a tin whistle as the gate reached three quarters of the way open and struggled on its mooring. He shut it behind him without much fanfare. The loose bolt on the gate made it lock itself. The sound of his footsteps then slightly varied in sound as his feet went from the outdoors to the lane. The wonders of science. He remembered how as a child he would stomp his feet wildly and be mesmerised by the changing sounds. He would jump as if on a trampoline till his knees couldn't take any more. These days his homecoming was a lot more subdued. The handle of the aluminium glass door crunched as he applied downward pressure. The featherweight door easily swung open as his chewed fingernails burrowed down to open the hard laces of his black school shoes. His moist socks hit the lino floor as he ghosted across the kitchen towards the hallway. The hall carpet providing a softer terrain as his footsteps sank into the floor for the remaining few yards to his room. His bedroom door was light and narrow with a loose handle. It breezed open as he entered and then shut it closed. Almost like someone shielding themselves with sheets of newspaper, it never felt private but right now, it was as good as it got. He slung his bag against the corner desk, threw his jacket on the hook on the door before collapsing prostrate on the bed.

He closed his eyes and just dreamed of blackness. He had an ambivalence towards his survival from a quasi-near-death experience. He wasn't particularly happy to still be alive but he didn't fancy death either. Not just yet. *'Something has to give'* he told himself. He felt something stirring deep within. The suppressed beast in his nature was beginning to get restless.

•

Flynn

Chapter Five: What Lies Beneath

The stand for "PLAYERS" society now loomed large. Flynn felt slightly more abrasion on the cobble lock beneath his feet. The dizziness subdued. Every one of the Players was dressed in a Bohemian manner, the table resembled some sort of fucked up fashion competition. Some of the lads had sports gear under brown leather jackets with cowboy boots and panama hats. Some girls had luminous tights with dark shawls and scraggy hair, slim girls with long skirts and "big units" with short skirts. On the face of it, it was a freak show, but a freedom underpinned by a want to be different. The Players were something very different but very beautiful.

The Players were a friendly bunch, anybody who paused momentarily at their stall was mobbed, "Hey you'd make a great actor, oh my god you have the best look ever!" They could really plámás every shape, size and creed of individual. True masters of their craft. Make everyone feel ten feet tall and they'll sign on the dotted line! A cheer would go up from the Players group every time a new member signed up. A celebration of fresh meat into their theatrical society.

Flynn then caught sight of him for the first time, sitting slightly aloof from the Players stand yet almost joined to them by an invisible umbilical cord, he was one of them yet looked like the most pissed off and disinterested man on Trinity campus. It was Hamish. He exuded the perfect air of a guy who just didn't give a fuck about what the world thought of him. Despite his brief of inveigling "freshers" to join this theatrical society, he was slumped on a chair oblivious to the noise, throngs and masses around him. With each roar and cacophony of noise Hamish became even more disdainful towards the table of Players beside him. He wore a three-quarter buttoned green duffle anorak, faded blue jeans and a pair of black and white retro Adidas shoes. Beneath the duffle anorak he wore a wine-coloured silk shirt with navy-blue cravat. He had square shoulders and a powerful build which was out of sync with his mostly non-athletic looking colleagues. His floppy ginger hair looked like he had given it two swipes of a comb in the morning and called it a day. A couple of days stubble adorned his well-chiselled and cinematic face. His idiosyncrasies carried an extraordinary magnetism. Inexplicably, people were just drawn to him, like a moth to the flame. Two unique and polar opposite worlds were about to collide.

A round girl with luminous green tights and a sheepskin jacket approached him with a beaming smile. She looked straight into Flynn's eyes and he couldn't help being drawn to her. "Hey! Did you ever dream of being an actor, you'd be awesome." There was an innocence of positivity in her approach, inviting him into their chaotic world where all freaks were welcome. "You'd have the best look ever for stage." Flynn was six foot two inches tall, he was well-built, but his lack of confidence meant he had always seemed smaller and more retracted. He even walked with a stoop to avoid interactions. He had always lived in the shadows. Survival, or so he thought. Despite his crouched stance he still towered over the round girl in luminous green tights and sheepskin jacket as she surveyed him up and down. He wore an orange lined green anorak with a silver zip on the sleeve, the coat was well weather beaten but at least the elements had taken the cheap, shiny look off it over time. Underneath he wore a plain white t-shirt with stone washed blue jeans and a pair of white converses. He had jet black hair which just seemed to shunt forward like a myriad of spider legs. But for his chronic demeanour, he would almost fit in. Round girl in luminous green tights wasn't going to be put off by anyone's demeanour. She was already surrounded by freaks and Flynn liked the look of this freak show. Back in St. Davids the freaks were pummelled, ostracised and lived in the shadows. Back in St. David's there was no gauntlet of diverse societies on their open day. Gaelic football or hurling was the height of the diversity on offer. After that, if you acted out of line, first prize was a box in the snot! Here they were celebrating freaks. Like the Red Army liberating Auschwitz, there was to be no oppression of freaks in Trinity, they obviously had a big enough population to support themselves. This was a different world to anything like Flynn had previously imagined. A celebration of their idiosyncrasies and a pride in projecting themselves as different. Happy to be the pariahs, rejecting mainstream and any semblance of acceptance.

"Okay," said Flynn. "Of course okay," said round girl in luminous green tights, "you'll be amaaaaaaazing, my name is Lydia and I look forward to seeing you around," pointing back at the stand towards a skinny girl with golden dreadlocks and shouts "Hey Tia, this gorgeous guy is going to be another Player." God love her purity of spirit and zeal. She ushers him across to the Players' table where the awaiting Tia was just as bullish and happy. "First time acting? " she asks Ehh… yeah it is," he replies as the grenadine filled his face from the shyness he had almost momentarily been distracted from. "The start of great things," she says as if acknowledging a patient in the nut house checking in for treatment. "… eh… sound…

thanks … can't wait," choked Flynn in a scarcely audible tone. To the left of the table sat Hamish, whose disinterested demeanour hadn't changed. Like a man stuck in purgatory, as if every sinew of this world bored him to tears. Perhaps that was his greatest asset. Hamish never valued anything and played like he'd nothing to lose.

Flynn's gaze was irrationally transfixed on Hamish. He sensed the dreadlocked Tia giving him a look of warning, puzzled at this infatuation. Flynn thanked Tia again and shuffled a few feet forward so that he was level with Hamish, as he passed by he heard Hamish speak in a quasi-cockney twang; "Fresh fuckin' fish!" Flynn didn't know but could only assume this derogatory term was directed at him on foot of the nerve-riddled deadbeat joining an actor's society. Flynn felt a heavy push in his back, it was Hamish. An all too familiar physical shove to let him know he didn't belong, he knew this well enough from St. Davids. However, something was very different this time. "Come on you miserable fuck, I'll show you around," said Hamish and brushed past him. He accelerated so quickly through the crowd that Flynn struggled to keep up. Flynn dodged and weaved whereas Hamish just bashed past people. Soon they were clear of the gauntlet and entered Front Square. The hood on Hamish' duffel anorak bobbed defiantly as he strode across Front Square with Flynn in pursuit.

"Right, let's get a can of lager in here first," said Hamish as he veered off to the left of Front Square, down the ramp and began a brief descent into the first of two student bars on Trinity campus called the Buttery. Two good-looking girls linking arms sauntered towards them. Obviously, locked in 'good-looking girl conversation' they stood squarely whilst maintaining each other's eye contact and therefore took up the full diameter of the ramp. As usual, they expected all subservient comers to yield way, however as Hamish trundled towards them Flynn realized this wasn't going to be the case. Hamish joined his two hands together as if in diving formation and theatrically drove his hands between the two girls breaking their arm link and casting them aside in one movement.

"Make a fuckin' hole ladies," as he bashed through the middle of them. Flynn was directly behind him like an inflatable banana being towed by a speed boat. He couldn't alter course. Guilty by association. Hamish was gone through the gap as Flynn turned to offer an apology. The impact had shocked both girls to the core. Their eyes in perfect symmetry seemed to narrow in anger and outrage as they closed in on Flynn. "Oh my god, what the fuck?" She was wearing a pink V-neck top with hugging tracksuit bottoms and UGG boots. Flynn was frozen to the spot but before she could get the second line out he felt the jolt of Hamish's grip pulling him down the ramp. "Open your fuckin' eyes next time, Sweetheart!" roared Hamish as he sucked Flynn through the outer door of Buttery. The girls stood still, flabbergasted on the ramp, their outrage growing.

The foyer of the Buttery was relatively spacious until entry into the dark chamber within. Claustrophobic buttresses and a low ceiling roof enhanced the cauldron effect. Hamish lit a cigarette upon entry and exhaled a giant plume of smoke in the faces of four lads seated beside the bar. *'Six cans of Miller for £5'* hung on a black sign above the bar, carved in chalk. Hamish threw a crumpled fiver note out of his jeans pocket in the direction of the bar counter. The note looked like a dead eel had rotted away. Hamish picked it up and began unfurling the note all the while inhaling and exhaling the cigarette hung on his lip.

"Now Sister! Get me six fuckin' cans, please." Hamish bellowed a laugh at the Nun on the Irish five pound note. Sister Catherine McAuley, founder of the Sisters of Mercy was now being used as a medium of currency for buying cans of Miller. "Barman," he yelped, "Six cans of Miller please." Flynn was still shook after the encounter a couple of minutes previously as Hamish slammed a can down beside him on the counter. "Here's to the fuckin' Sisters of Mercy!" he bellowed another extravagant laugh. Hamish tapped his fingernail three times on the pop-top of the Miller can before flicking it backwards in the same movement. He air toasted Flynn and flung the can towards his mouth at an almost 90-degree angle tilting his head back until his face was almost perpendicular with the ceiling. Freakishly, the only thing facing Flynn was his stubbled chin and the navy-blue cravat which drifted around his neck at this gargantuan swallow. "Warm and tastes like piss but it's still fuckin' refreshing Matey." Hamish returned the gravity of his head to its axis and looked at Flynn, the froth from the Miller can still residing on his lips. "Well come on then, drink up Princess!" Flynn was still holding his can in his right hand - still unopened. Unsure of himself. Hamish slapped him on the shoulder "Giddy up!" Flynn looked at Hamish and quickly decided that this chance encounter wouldn't last long unless he engaged with the frolics of his newfound friend. The cans were warm, obviously the cheap drink deal didn't include refrigeration. Flynn didn't tap the pop-top with the expertise of Hamish and instead just flipped the lid which resulted in gushing froth over himself and the floor. He sensed himself being looked at. *'Fuck it, just drink it, Flynn.'* He tilted his head back and felt the lukewarm frothy Miller roll down his throat as the fizz stung his tonsils. He recoiled once the stinging sensation became overwhelming and felt the backwashing of fizzy beer in his nostrils almost suffocating him. He looked at Hamish and tried to keep a straight face.

"There ye go Tiger!" said Hamish as he relaxed back against the bar with his left elbow. He flipped off his duffel coat which he consigned to the nearest bar stool and pulled out his cigarettes. White box with a gold king label, Marlboro Lights were his brand. He flicked open the top of the box with his right hand and retracted his left hand towards his mouth. With great dexterity, the new cigarette was affixed perfectly to his lips before another combustion was accompanied by a long inhalation.

Hamish exhaled a giant plume of smoke as he looked at Flynn properly for the first time. Flynn was on edge, shifting his weight from foot to foot as he peered nervously from under his eyelids. He fumbled nervously with his Miller can as perspiration gripped his skin. Hamish cast a disdainful look in his direction, "so are you fuckin' autistic?" he asked. The depth and incision of the question cut deep inside. It also sparked the embers of a rage inside Flynn. "To be honest, I may as well be fuckin' autistic," replied Flynn as he took a giant gulp of warm brew. "What's with all the fuck-up red face and trembling hands? Ye know my Grandad had Parkinson's, he used to shake like that before he died. Shuffling around the place as his faculties shut down. He was eighty-fuckin'-six though." Hamish was confrontational and in no mood for some blabbering mess.

Flynn

Flynn looked Hamish in the eyes for the first time. It was like looking at the snaked headed 'Medusa'. Flynn felt his eyeballs melting, as if Hamish was looking into his soul. His perspiration exploded to saturation. His t-shirt became moist to the touch. The dormant beast inside Flynn was being gently prodded by this interrogation. Hamish dove into this cigarette packet and emerged with another smoke which he shoved unceremoniously into Flynn's mouth, "Here have one of them, it might smoke out some of the snakes in your gut," he flashed him a psychotic grin. Flynn loved the analogy of snakes inside him. It was exactly how he felt in public, being consumed by venomous reptiles which sucked the life out of him. Flynn wasn't a smoker. His previous couple of tokes had given him head spins and vomiting. He took the cigarette as it saved him talking. Hamish lit up his smoke and he inhaled. The sensation of the burning flax paper followed as nicotine infused smoke bellowed down his windpipe and waged war on his alveoli. It was a deep and intense inhalation. The sort that would topple a novice smoker. He shot through another couple of deep inhalations in quick succession which almost burnt the cigarette down to the orange speckled filter. The vision of smoking out the snakes had consumed him. "Easy Tiger! That's some hoover you've got." said Hamish with a laugh. The backdraught wasn't long in coming. Delayed reaction. "Oh, Holy Jaysus!" said Flynn as a tsunami of dizziness swept over him. The Buttery turned into a disco ball. "Mind the King Lear's, I'm off to the Khazi," said Hamish with another chuckle. Flynn grabbed the bar counter for dear life. He felt like a guinea pig for NASA. The bar began to swing from side to side. Entranced by the thoughts of the snakes, Flynn sucked down even harder on the filter. The burning sensation on his lips halted his gallop as he had smoked through the filter. A couple of minor burn blisters decorated his fingers. If the first reaction was delayed, then this was like the toppling of the Taj Mahal. The bar began doing somersaults as the contents of the hallucinogenic dam washed over him. The crazy buttresses spun violently above his head. Black speckles obscured his vision and his stomach served notice of evacuation. His knuckles turned white. His drowning man's grip on the bar counter began to loosen as perspiration greased the traction between his hands and the polished mahogany counter. He increased power to his hands but the film of sweat countered the force of his grip. He looked downwards towards the sticky tiled floor but his perception of looking downwards soon became skywards. He lost his grip on the bar counter and slumped to one knee as a discreet slingshot of vomit catapulted out of his mouth. *'Get up Flynn! Back on your fuckin' feet, you're making a show of us.'*

Another ignominious fall in the life and times of Daryl Flynn. Even a seasoned smoker with tar coated alveoli wouldn't try to inhale a full cigarette in a few long drags. *'What the fuck am I doing?'* He looked back towards the bar which transitioned from floor to ceiling in a blur. He scraped back to his feet and grabbed a hold of a buttress, a temporary life buoy. The embarrassment blitzed any pain as all the blood in his body seemed to migrate at once to his face and head. Nobody seemed to take much notice of his slip. He wiped his mouth and dabbed his forehead with a napkin from the counter. A few sniggers and few whispers from the side tables but it seemed the concentration of the Buttery world was elsewhere. He had got away with it. The room slowly began to right itself before his eyes. Flynn's only thought was focused on the 'snakes' inside him and smoking them out. He could probably drown the bastards as well. He took a long agricultural gulp of his warm can, the warm fizz acting in perfect symmetry with the smoke inhalation. He put his elbow on the bar as a further anchor, the wet counter formed a liquid poultice with his elbow.

Hamish came bounding back around the corner, a big grin on his face. "Great trout in here today Matey!" he paused as he looked at Flynn's face, first signs of battle scars after his mini-meltdown. "That's a nice ghosty you've got going on there!" Hamish's eyes widened as he reached and lit up another smoke. "How are your reptile friends doing there?" as he probed a finger into Flynn's gut, laughing. He had a certain mesmeric way about him, a unique magnetism. Flynn laughed, "I'll smoke the bastards out yet, might be no harm to drown them as well," as he pole-axed the remaining contents of this second can. He felt something stirring deep in his soul, something unconnected to the guise he currently kept. It was the first time he felt the beast in his nature beginning to emerge.

The warm Miller. Flynn was more a can of cider or flagon of cider man. His drinking before this was limited to his cousin John and best pal Finbar in St. Anne's Park. Outcasts murdering a few cans. Finbar's sister Aisling was friends with Rachel. They would sometimes tag along. *'Outcasts Anonymous.'* That's where he had met Rachel, far down the rung of the Raheny social food chain. Just where he belonged. The conversation thus far was a damp squib. Hamish looked disinterested from the get go but at least now he had the consolation of warm cans of Miller. He pointed his can back towards himself "Anyway I'm Hamish, and you are?" he held up his can in front of Flynn as if beckoning to write his name on a piece of paper and post it through the top of his can. "I'm Daryl… eh… Daryl Flynn," he said with hesitation, his name sounded strange now when he said it out loud. It further deepened the hatred of himself. "Daryl Fuckin' Flynn! Well, it's a pleasure to meet you," said Hamish as he extended his hand forward in a vice-grip handshake, slightly lubricated by Miller and sweat. Flynn felt the pain of his metacarpals being crushed. The pain prodded the beast inside him a little more. Hamish smiled as he squeezed and jacked up the pressure on Flynn's hand. "Come on, Darren, shake hands like a man!" he teased. "It's fuckin' Daryl" Flynn barked back as he upped the ante of his own, he too had a bear like grip and turned the tables on Hamish. Defiance, albeit mini defiance. Hamish let go. It was as if he was managing some form of exorcism on Flynn. Probing and cajoling the beast within, as if he had some sort of sixth sense that Flynn wanted nothing more than Hara-kiri to liberate himself and unleash his demons. "That's the spirit soldier!" as he threw back his head with a laugh and clinked glasses. The beast was beginning to emerge from the darkness inside.

Flynn

Chapter Six: Moby Dick and The Adulterer

Rachel was going through sustained hell. There was no reprieve from her demons within. The demons which not only fuelled her depression but had also dragged her into the depths of an eating disorder. She had blown up in the Leaving Cert, capable of so much more. The demons struck, again. Her overall points tally precipitated her enrolment in a Post Leaving Certificate course in Crumlin College, a token IT course that she hated from day one. Finbar's sister Aisling was her best friend and confidant but she had gone off to University College Galway to study some Biomedical Science course. Either way, she was pretty much gone out of her life. Apart from the token text message and call you could see she had found her niche down in Galway and was moving on with her life. The dichotomy of having Aisling moving forwards as she was dragged backwards into mediocrity aroused feelings of bitterness towards her and everything around her. She had gradually withdrawn contact from Aisling, sick of hearing about new friends and how she was getting on with her life. It felt the whole world was simply passing her by. Day one in Crumlin College she felt unbelievably self-conscious, it was as if the walls were talking about "the size of yer one" or "jaysus that's some hoop." She had heard all the hurtful torments during her school years being called "the pig" and "the pudding" and "a big unit." She held out hope that once school was over, life would be different, a new beginning away from the bullies. Open water where she could start afresh, a new identity, a new mind, even a new body. Now the rat trap had closed in and she was paralysed by anxiety, fear and depression. She gradually began to retract from Crumlin College and her absenteeism began to accelerate.

Flynn

She sought solace in junk food. Always on her own. Always in the dark, where she wouldn't have to see her own reflection. Incessant movies, the scarier or more impactful, the better. Anything to black out the demonic thoughts from her psyche for a few hours. She still worked a few hours in the Cineplex in Coolock, ironically selling popcorn and sweets to movie goers. A dead end. She was metamorphosing into a whale. Even her skin became scaly from the bad diet and junk food. There was no word from Flynn. She had texted him and tried to reach out. The only person whoever seemed to be nice to her or form a connection with her. The horrible bastard even told her he loved her. All manipulation. All those clandestine meetings and for what? To satisfy his sexual gratification because she was a loser that would accede to his every request. The weak preying on the weaker.

Her last rendezvous with Flynn accelerated her feelings of depression and anxiety. She made a big effort for him. She really liked him and like many girls dreamed of making him her life partner. She could sense a darkness deep within his soul. She wanted them to confront their demons together. There was a period of her life where she ventured into positivity, looking towards the future with hope. If they both got a good Leaving Cert, they could move on to college and leave the past behind. Leave behind their troubles and build a future together. Flynn would never acknowledge her in public but that was OK with her. She knew his chronic nerves and lack of confidence wouldn't allow him to express any public affection. Walking down the street hand in hand was a Utopian ideal when it came to Daryl Flynn.

Flynn

She was living off scraps. Clandestine rendezvous' and the odd few cans when herself and Aisling would hook up with himself and Finbar. She could always see the darkness within when she looked into his eyes. It was an impenetrable darkness. How can someone love you if they won't let you into their soul? Any deep or meaningful conversation was met by a stone wall. Flynn would retreat to his sanctuary of his dark pit.

Occasionally, she wondered if knowing the turmoil inside someone else just garnered resentment. It was their last meet up in St. Annes that changed things, he had told her he loved her. It was premeditated emotional blackmail. He had taken her virginity and it was far from cinematic. It was manipulation of the mind, preying on her love for him. *'Who the fuck wanted to lose their virginity beside a fuckin' playground?'* But it was the manner of execution. The aggression running wild through his body as he turned her around and penetrated her, it felt like slaughter in an abattoir. On the night in question they met at the same spot by the west gate. The conversation always started out the same, questions about why he never acknowledged her in public and did he see her as just some easy mooch? Flynn would always cover his tracks and trot out a line about being private, not wanting anyone to know his business. She liked him, always made a considerable effort to look nice, teenage perfume and DIY tanning. It still didn't cover up the fact that she wasn't a looker. She wasn't relationship material in Flynn's eyes. The burden of being with a fellow loser would further reaffirm to the world his status. This was a one-way street. He would use her and didn't really care if she never spoke to him again or not. But she kept coming back.

Flynn

They walked towards the playground, impending sexual gratification. He felt his heart starting to accelerate in his chest. This was routine. They would kiss and then he would pull her close and put his hands under her top, glide them up her back and undo the hooks on her bra. There was never any resistance as his hands slid along her skin. The touch of flesh with a burgeoning erection gave him a burning arousal. He also carried the added adrenaline of the 'fear of getting caught.' This was not a girl to brag about, try get your pleasure and brush it all under the carpet. He would always start with her left nipple, enveloping an inch in diameter. He loved hearing her increased aspiration and soft moaning. Pleasurable pain. Once the right nipple had been equally satisfied, he ushered her hands down to his belt as she negotiated the liberation of his erection. Flynn then followed suit and exposed her sensory pleasure island as his fingers became moist. This was their routine, but tonight was different. Tonight, Flynn wanted to penetrate her. Immediately he noticed hesitation on Rachel's face. The look that says 'this has to mean something'.

"I love you" rolled off his tongue. She nodded reticently, as if still caught up in the pleasure and just hearing what she wanted to hear. She consented as she turned and gripped the black wired fence. It was sloppy and awkward. After much probing, he finally penetrated Rachel. Virginity lost, but she was still nothing to him. He didn't climax inside her. Instead, he pulled out and she made him climax as usual. After ejaculation and seconds of prolonged pleasure, Rachel, once again, became an irrelevance. "Let's get back it's getting cold," said Flynn, he looked at her with ruthless shark eyes. Rachel dutifully pulled her clothes back on. Flynn wanted to get as far away from her as possible. He had just told her he loved her and now after the deed was done, he wanted to get the hell away from her. There was never a thought about how this might affect her. How this would affect Rachel's confidence and self-esteem mattered nothing to him. He thought about how the lads would refer to her as a pig. Flynn never wanted to see her again. And he never would, alive.

Rachel thought that her sacrifice would bring them closer together. Somehow bring him out of himself and unleash the demons within. But after it was over there was no embrace, no sensual kiss, no sense of bonding. They walked back together, he had made reference to the cold but maybe it was the cold inside his heart. There was a token parting kiss before they reached the exposure of street lights. It was a cursory meeting of their lips, almost as if he was pulling away before the engagement. She barely tasted his saliva. He walked away quietly and didn't look back. She stood and looked after him hoping for a return glance but he disappeared under the street lights. He hugged the shadows as he made a turn for home, his shoulders slumped to avoid detection. She had texted him that night that she loved him and was there for him. She texted him the next morning, the next afternoon and the next evening before her shift in the Cineplex in Coolock. She checked her phone every few minutes, but no text ever arrived. Waiting for Godot. Perhaps Flynn had no credit. Surely, those interactions meant something to him.

After days of unrequited texts it became clear that maybe he needed space. Maybe next time he drank cider with Finbar a text would come through looking for a hook-up. Anything to stay in his life. She could make this work, keep chipping away at the rubble of his hurt till she found herself inside his heart. She had contemplated going to his house, the desperation to look into his eyes. She might see something inside him, then let him know she understood him and was there for him. She remembers getting dressed for work one evening and something breaking inside her as she looked at herself in the mirror. She looked like Moby Dick in a waistcoat, she had ballooned. The blue waistcoat was at its limit and certainly wouldn't close, pockets of fat protruding from underneath her short sleeves. Putting on her work slacks was like squeezing a slug into a slot machine. She made eye contact with herself, the sort that either makes or breaks a human being. It was only a matter of time.

Her father Terry was having no such trouble in inveigling romance. He was having an affair with a widow from the Five Lamps, Grace Farrell. He met her in Graingers Pub on Talbot street several years previously. A retirement bash for one of the lads from the bus depot on a Sunday night. He was locked drunk and she was desperate, a match made in heaven. It was a one-night thing but became the perfect hook up. Grace was vulnerable and in need of company. She was approaching fifty and her self-esteem was on the floor. The kids were grown up and the family had splintered. She worked as a cleaner around offices in the IFSC and lived in the shadows. She could actually go from one end of the day to the next without speaking a word to anyone. So much so that the majority of office workers actually assumed she was a foreigner. She lived on Shamrock Terrace, a gritty boulevard of the beautiful inner city. Some evenings she would come in the door and forget to eat. She would chain-smoke cigarettes till the appetite was suppressed. She drank till she fell asleep and the next day she got up and worked. Years of hardship was written across her face but she could do herself up "a bit of blond colour and a bit of slap." Terry became a life raft. Something to look forward to, perhaps a life companion. Simple things. The odd meal out and the odd few drinks. Someone to break the loneliness of the house. Terry told her everything she wanted to hear. He told her it would take time. But in the end they would be together. He was the master at exploiting weaknesses. A parasite.

He would call over after his shifts and drink coffee, tell her what she needed to hear to finally get her undressed. His advances were basic and blunt to the point of caveman tactics, "Well Gracie, jaysus you're looking well, who's my number one gal?" He would lean in and kiss her. She would always offer the same resistance: "ye keep telling me we're going out for a meal and a few drinks or a weekend away but there's no sign of nothing."

"Sure jaysus, Love, Rome wasn't built in a day, a lot of what I'm doing is behind the scenes and centred on building a future for the two of us together." He would pause and look into her eyes, "Ye know I love ye, now come here to me you." He would grab her in a playful wrestling hold until she giggled and laughed. "Ah, there ye are now, there's my Gracie!" Once she was laughing he was winning. He'd run his hand up her thigh and once she offered no resistance, he was home free. He'd pull her off the couch and relocate to her bedroom getting undressed along the way. She would lie back on the bed and allow him to slide off her knickers. Some days he would barrel straight into it, but others demanded more subtlety. "Go down on me Terry will ye!" she would say. This irked him slightly as it meant a delay to him getting through the door of the Watermill. But needs must. "Of course, my love, now get ready for some 'Terry Luvin'." He always knew how close she was to climax by how tightly she gripped his hair. He would then ramp up the intensity even more as her fingers dug into his scalp and she began moaning loudly. Her breathing would accelerate, elongated wheezes from the chain-smoking. Once her body started trembling he knew she was close. "Ah, holy fuckin' jaysus, Terry!" she would say as she accelerated down the runway for final departure. A loud exhalation and even louder scream accompanied the orgasmic catharsis. She would then slump almost lifeless and limp back on the bed as she recovered her breathing. Open season for Terry to have his merry way with her. "Terry Luvin" was a guerilla warfare approach to sex, get in, get orgasmic and get out of there. He would penetrate her with long deep thrusts and bring himself to climax within minutes. Every so often they would swap position, other times he would be aroused enough to barrel into her. There was no second bullet in the gun of "Terry Luvin", once he had climaxed that was him done. He would then hold her tightly for several moments, savouring the post orgasmic connection before his brain would immediately revert to 'evacuation mode'. An erect penis with no conscience. He lived in his own micro-universe, a bubble of ruthless self gratification. It was now a game of expedition to the Watermill. Grace just wanted to be held, someone to wrap their arms around her and make her feel loved. "Jaysus! Where does the time go to, Gracie," he would never say he was heading off to get pissed.

Terry loved the challenge of the post intercourse dialogue, a further extension of his manipulation skills. It was meat and drink for him but keeping a straight face was sometimes difficult. He always had a cover story. He often talked about his volunteer work with the St. Vincent de Paul. "Jaysus, Gracie, if only ye knew how tough some young people have it out there in Dublin." He would often pause for dramatic effect, mid-sentence, and allow his voice to quiver. "Keeping the young people going means the world to me." A master manipulator.

Grace would rub his back slowly, offering comfort at his disingenuous outpourings. "Terry…" she would softly whisper, "you're so good to give your time for the people who need it most." She would rest her head on his back and embrace him. Some days Terry felt like bursting out laughing mid-monologue, but he always checked himself. He felt it would be better not to lose this little hook up. He embellished his soccer career to the point that Grace believed he was a professional at the highest level. He could freely drop all the big names in conversation knowing full well Grace knew nothing about football. His depiction of himself as a sporting hero created an even greater allure for her.

She rarely socialised and Terry always demanded that she keep their relationship a secret "until the time was right," he used to glow, "and then we will tell the world together Gracie, I can't wait to tell everyone how much I'm in love with you." She often wanted to break ranks and tell someone, anyone, that she was with a famous footballer. No doubt it would make them look at her differently. But she had long decided to hold her counsel lest it jeopardise their love.

Terry would also talk about the team he was coaching, he would carefully choreograph his struggles with phantom players and how being head coach could be hugely stressful. "I'll be off now to training, ye know me, I have to be the first one to arrive, ye always have to lead by example" he would say, "Love you very much, Gracie." The door would close behind him and silence would descend. The next sounds would be Grace pouring herself a large gin and the flick of the flint wheel of her lighter. She would sit in silence chain-smoking, dreaming of the future. Every so often she allowed herself a grin and a chuckle as she thought about the love she had for Terry Reilly.

Flynn

Chapter Seven: Men of the Cloth

Flynn always wondered why they targeted him. *'Did they have a network of intel, a system of psychometric analysis?'* A bastard child from a broken home with a promiscuous mother. *'How did they know he would keep his mouth shut?'* The piercing memories of The Vestry where it all happened, the glacial expression of the Sacristan as he left. Weekday masses were the most dangerous, the days when he would be on his own. At least at the weekend there were three of four other altar boys, strength in numbers as such. But the early morning masses he was a sitting duck. The local parish priest advised his mother to get Flynn into the church from an early age after the passing of his father. "Bring him closer to God and help him develop his spiritual wellbeing."

Flynn remembered the priest sitting at the table drinking tea and eating Custard Cream biscuits. *'Custard Fuckin' Creams.'* He recalled the tension in the house before the big visit. The cleaning, the hoovering, the washing windows, all to mark the great arrival of this mythological figure. The man of the cloth. The pillar of the community, an extension of this *'loving God.'* Flynn was told to sit at the table and "shut your fuckin' mouth." Under no circumstances were kids allowed to address a priest. Flynn remembered every detail of the visit, the towering figure decked out in impeccable black vestments rounded off with the white collar. Intimidation personified, as if somehow this man was the key-holder to heaven and hell. The stale scent of incense and cigarettes. He took his place at the table and spoke sternly to Flynn's mother. He told her Flynn should report to the Vestry five times a week to serve as an altar boy. He scoffed his way through the triangular sandwiches his mother had prepared before devouring the Custard Creams. Flynn noted how he slurped his tea and spat crumbs from his mouth as he surveyed Flynn up and down. "He's a fine young boy. We will make a man of him Mrs. Flynn."

As the years went by Flynn theorised that it was fear which allowed the church to walk all over its people. He remembered how it was mostly the elderly who attended the early morning masses. Many of whom were hunchbacked and on their last legs. All of whom held a common theme, hopeful ascension through the pearly gates of the afterlife. Flynn had overheard elderly widows being coerced into leaving their estates to the church. All in return for the promise of eternal prayers. Fear triumphed and the widows were carted off to the boneyard nonetheless. Flynn had lived his whole life consumed by fear. His fear was real. He was a bastard child who didn't fit in. His environment strangled the life out of him. He became self-conscious and self-loathing. He sometimes thought about his own death. *'Who would actually give a fuck after Daryl Flynn was lowered beneath the earth?'* Perhaps death would be the ultimate release.

It didn't start straight away. They seemed to size him up during the first few weeks. A litmus test to see how vulnerable he truly was. Four priests were assigned to the local church. One of whom was just back from the missions in Africa. *'God help those poor Africans'*, Flynn often thought to himself, *'what he must have done to them over there…'* Flynn would arrive on his bicycle every morning at half-seven to get ready for eight o'clock mass. He would chain his bike to the railings and knock at the Vestry door where the Sacristan would let him in. The Sacristan's name was Brendan, as Flynn often heard the priests addressing him. He would never speak to Flynn, he might grunt at him but no more. He shuffled around like some freakish version of Frankenstein, with his long-boned, hollowed out face and constant dark rings around his eyes. He was like a phantom and would ghost through walls. He would always disappear once mass ended, leaving Flynn alone with whatever priest was serving.

The first time it happened stuck with him. An addendum of the misery he was living in but nothing more. Flynn noticed an upturn in the priest's mood that morning as mass had ended. It was followed by an invitation to his private chamber to help him with his vestments. He coaxed him inside and closed the door. Flynn thought it strange that he affixed the second bolt. The priest smoked a cigarette as he stalked Flynn who stood there with a mixture of fear and reverence. This was the Catholic Church. He made it ceremonial, almost ritualistic. *'The filthy fuckin' bastard'* coating him with something resembling Vaseline which was topped up by his spittle. "Now good man, don't make a sound." Flynn remembered feeling powerless as his trousers were removed and his backside exposed. He was frozen in paralysed shock. He remembered the feeling of penetration which made him sick to his stomach, the horrific pain in his rectum and lower abdomen. Two giant hands clasped around his shoulders. The sounds of grunting and heavily wheezed smoker breath on the back of his neck. His eyes watered and tears flowed as he tried to do what he was told, to not "make a sound." He clenched his teeth so hard he thought his gums would explode. He had bitten his tongue, a speckle landed on the ground in front of him. He focused on that speckle as best he could as his eyes watered and blurred his vision. The grunting accelerated, it was like the animalistic sounding of a wild boar. The thrusts to his rear end decreased as the priest seemed to collapse on top of his back. After a few seconds, he relinquished his grip and Flynn felt a release from the striking pain in his abdomen. "Good man, Daryl, take a biscuit for yourself there on the way out." He sparked up another cigarette and made some sort of blessing gesture. Almost as if to lure Flynn into the further fabrication that somehow this was holy liturgy which had just taken place. The bolt on the door was undone, "now run along and have a good day in school, good man."

Flynn remembered the icy winds as he cycled to school that day. He knew he had been violated but his trauma morphed into an acceptance. It came as no surprise. Even God was conspiring against Daryl Flynn. He retreated into a darker place. He became a ghost. Indifferent to life or death. Two orphaned children had begun serving mass around that time. They were boarders in the local school run by the Christian brothers. Flynn would observe fresh bruises on their bodies with regular occurrence. *'What hell were they going through?'* At least he could return to his council house and retreat to his box room. *'Those poor bastards had to live through even worse. Drunken beatings and round the clock violations.'* He often wondered where they ended up in life. *'More than likely they were strung out on drugs somewhere, destitute or dead.'* Flynn always remembered contrite absolution during mass:

"May God Almighty have mercy on us,
Forgive us our sins,
And bring us to everlasting life.
Amen."

Flynn

Flynn wondered when God would strike. Surely vengeance was on the cards from high above. Weeks, months and years passed by and Flynn still saw the priests, seemingly unchecked by the higher power. He resolved himself that one day he would take matters into this own hands. Another seed of darkness had been sewn within his soul.

Flynn

Chapter Eight: Bar Fight

Hamish looked around the room, an ominous air of madness filled his eyes. He looked at the table of four lads with the GAA gear bags. He had intentionally blown smoke in their faces on the way in. Flynn could see them eyeing him up too. They seemed like his best bet for an altercation. He metronomically flushed back another can down the hatch. "Get another twist in here, Matey! I'm off to pick a fight." Flynn wondered what sort of maniac he had got himself mixed up with. The incarnation of the wild man of Borneo with some crazed thirst for violence. Why on earth would he want to go starting fights in "freshers" week? He wasn't about to stiff Hamish on the drinks for fear of reprisal but made a mental note to himself that he should polish off the next few cans and head for higher ground. He felt trouble on the horizon. That scent of overcharged testosterone when all hell is about to break loose. He was never one for confrontation. The thoughts of it made him sick.

Hamish flanked around the side of the bar, a wry smile decorating his face. He breezed past the group of four lads "Good afternoon, Ladies… did you all get lost trying to find the Gay Bar?" with a further exhalation of his cigarette. The early pursuit of chaos had begun. The lad with the shaved head jumped to his feet incensed and ready for battle, beside him sat a more tanned chap with a V-neck jumper who also stood up with an icy stare. "Get the fuck back here ye ginger fuck!" shouted "shaved head man". Hamish kept walking and disappeared around the corner. Perhaps he just wanted to bring the lads to the precipice of conflict before pulling back. And why would you be bothered taking on four big lads with GAA gear bags, surely there were softer targets out there? Hamish disappeared down the far end of the Buttery. Luckily, the four lads didn't pursue him and settled back down, still incensed, however. Flynn felt their eyes burning a hole in the back of his head. Guilty by association. Just his luck. The visualisation swept over him of copping a hiding on the first day of "freshers" week on foot of this maniac going off on one. This was after all Trinity College, not the Lebanon.

Flynn chugged another long draught of warm Miller. The anxiety of impending conflict had moistened his palms. *'Fuck it.'* He reached across and grabbed Hamish's Marlboro Lights and stuck one in his mouth. He had no lighter. Hamish obviously took it with him. *'Bollix.'* He would have to interact with someone. Or he could wait for Hamish. *'Ah jaysus it's only asking for a light'* he told himself. The Miller raced around his insides. It was doing a fine job of nullifying the senses, of drowning some of the "snakes". The bar was horse-shoe in shape and could be approached from either side. He chose the clockwise direction away from the four lads. He spotted an immediate target. Two girls sat facing each other beneath the shaded buttress arch of the wall. Both were smoking and locked in intense conversation. So intense that neither altered their gaze as Flynn approached the table. Stammering slightly, "Eh mmm, could I have a light please"? Without breaking stride in conversation, one of the girls simply extended her left arm directly towards him. She held a silver zippo lighter in a tripod grip between her ring, middle and index finger of her left hand. Flynn took it from her grasp, it was quite heavy and had the name "Sarah" emblazoned with a lightning logo. The Zippo carried a warmth, a mixture of recently used lighter fluid with the heat from her finger grip and a microscopic film of perspiration. She obviously held this Zippo as a comfort twitch during conversation. Flynn delicately slid back the lid and exposed the spark wheel. He felt the slim moisture around the wheel bearing as he sharply flicked his thumb in a downward motion creating combustion. He slowly lifted the Zippo up to his cigarette, the crunching noise of flax paper followed by the taste of torched nicotine. She still held her arm outstretched with her fingers perfectly positioned in tripod format. The gaze from her friend had not altered during this hiatus. Flynn slid the lighter back in her pre-made finger perch. "Thanks," he said. She waved him away in token recognition, he wandered back to his spot at the counter. Zero eye contact, but at least he got a light.

Flynn parked himself back at his mini conclave at the bar counter. For the moment he was on his own. He wondered if Hamish had simply fucked off and left him with his thumb stuck in the dam. Surely, those lads would have no interest in giving him a beating for the sake of it. He inhaled strongly, like an asthmatic frantically puffing an inhaler in the middle of a violent attack. He felt the smoke rebounding from the pit of his lungs before bouncing back up his windpipe. The back of his throat felt like dry season in the Serengeti. He drained back another helping of Miller which tasted more and more like sparkling jacuzzi water but anything to irrigate the senses. The nicotine catapulted its way around his body, switching off one light switch at a time. His skin began to crawl and he could feel a numbness in his face. He took another gulp of his can, in an effort to rebalance a capsizing boat. *'Fuck it. Sure, what harm?'* A certain "fuck you" to the demons inside him who had created this anxiety-ridden deadbeat. Flynn dragged even deeper this time, the room began another rotation. He felt a rebelliousness inside this stomach, the bile and other components were getting antsy. The beast started to flex its muscles. There was a cathartic feeling inside Flynn as his body involuntarily started to wage a civil war within. An ironic smile crossed his face, at least he wasn't shuffling nervously and perspiring profusely trying to make awkward small talk. Another heave of warm Miller down his throat. The sense of violent illness was beginning to plateau, he still felt sick, but it was manageable, as if the nicotine inside his system was just tickling nerve endings. Still no sign of Hamish. He cast a quick glance over his shoulder to the table of lads who returned daggers. Perfect. He raided Hamish's box of cigarettes again, using the ember of his dying butt to spark up a new smoke, a flash of ingenuity and saving himself another trip over to tripod girl. A blanking avoided.

His throat raged war, red raw, he necked back the rest of his final can and then felt compelled to get another twist. He leaned over the bar counter, elevating himself slightly on his elbows. He grabbed the attention of the nearest barman, who happened to be the token bandana clad hippy, always the compulsory addition to every student bar. Bandana hippy man looked like the world was his oyster as he served students with glee, no doubt nicely imbued with a steady consumption of marijuana to uphold his relaxed, happy-go-lucky demeanour. He looked at Flynn with far away eyes. "Howya! Can I have six of them Millers please, bud," he followed this utterance by a giant cough as he tried to hock up his tonsil to give it some moisture. His delivery of speech was improving. Bandana hippy man duly obliged and dispatched himself to the back of the bar where he retrieved a four pack and then bizarrely reached into the fridge for the other two. Flynn counted out five punt coins, four shiny and one slightly weather-beaten. He arranged them on top of each other with the red deer on top and the Viking boat on the bottom. God forbid he might be questioned on the quality of his legal tender. He placed the small stack on the black marble counter, slightly submerged by the spillage from clumsy bar staff and students alike. Bandana hippy man scooped the five coins up in his hand and threw them straight in the till. No need for an abacus and the trade was complete. Now for the next dilemma, to drink the ice-cold cans first or the ones that felt like they had been sitting on a radiator. Flynn's throat offered a veto of the temporary embargo of the warm cans. Unlike its warm cousin, the sound of the ice-cold can top opening was more clinical and unleashed a soft plume of gas. It also didn't spray everyone within a two-metre radius upon discharge. The sensation of ice-cold beer down his throat was the perfect catharsis. Time to commit another bombing raid on Hamish's Marlboro Lights. Bit by bit he was starting to feel less like Daryl Flynn.

Hamish bounded back around the corner with great gusto and abandon. "Sorry about that, Matey, had to drop a few Cosbys off at the pool!" He regained his perfect perch and threw a cigarette onto his lips. *'Jaysus ye can't go around saying things like that'* he thought to himself. *'Had this fella just escaped from the Grange Gorman Nuthouse?'* Hamish looked across at the table of lads and beamed them a big smile. He gestured a mock *'panzy-boy'* wave in their direction.

The Buttery was beginning to fill up at this stage, so the antics of Hamish had somewhat blended into the jungle of students getting pissed. However, his antics had not gone unnoticed by the four lads, two of whom were McEntyres from South Armagh, Rory and Seán. Rory sported a shaved head and his tanned associate was his cousin, Seán, sporting the V-neck jumper. Flynn saw out of the corner of his eye the four lads at the table get up to leave and grab their gear bags. *'Thank Christ'* he said to himself. *'Disaster avoided.'* Until he saw an ominous grin across Hamish's face. 'Please don't say anything, please don't say anything.' "Bye, Bye Ladies," sneered Hamish as he leaned back on the bar counter and smiled towards the four lads. Rory was the spiritual leader of the group and wasn't about to take any more messing. He made a beeline for Hamish, "What did you say ye arrogant ginger Proddie fuck?" Flynn felt that sinking feeling - he couldn't handle conflict. That familiar feeling descended. Almost as if he was drowning, his lungs filling up with water.

Rory McEntyre, son of one of the biggest property developers in Ireland and the UK. His father, Rory Senior, was actually published on Ireland's rich list several years in a row. He was also known for staunch republican leanings and question marks had always remained about how he built up the empire so quickly. The McEntyre family was not one to be messed with. McEntyre shaped up to Hamish who was still slouched against the bar completely relaxed, in almost a state of Zen. The blue pigmentation of Hamish's eyes registered no fear whatsoever, a defiant grin adorned his face as he looked straight ahead. His brain obviously so comfortably imbalanced by fight neurons that the thoughts of impending violence couldn't so much as trigger nervous anxiety. McEntyre leaned in towards him, "Let's take a wee walk, ye ginger fuck!" This wasn't his first rodeo. He was flanked either side by his three comrades, almost in perfect synchronisation. "Excellent idea," retorted Hamish, "and is it OK if I bring my friend, Darren?" he ventured further. Flynn grimaced but stood passively, like a victim of locked-in syndrome, thoughts flooded back of his last conflict with Reilo. Staring at the ground had served him well.

The warm Miller and nicotine was still doing a merry dance inside his body, almost beckoning his adrenaline gland to *'please start working.'* The beast was beginning to stir but years of Daryl Flynn failures and crippling nerves still left him bereft of any fire. He had met Hamish less than an hour ago and every minute was like a white-knuckle ride. Now he had brought violence to his door and an impending beating on his first day in Trinity. "Easy now, sweetheart, don't get your knickers in a twist, you and your little boyfriends just run along and go straight home to your Mum." Nobody called out Rory McEntyre. He was the alpha male. Through status, money, brains and his own physical toughness, he instilled fear and respect in others without engagement. To be somehow targeted by some extravagant ginger-headed, English geezer with a cravat and wine silk shirt was an outrage.

McEntyre darted out his right hand in a claw like fashion and gripped Hamish's cravat. He shunted him forwards towards the Buttery door. His henchmen beckoned Flynn to follow, he acquiesced. Fear. The blood vessels on Hamish's neck began to contort as the oxygen supply was being cut off but his grin remained. "And when you go home to your Mum be sure and tell your sister I said hello as well," answered Hamish defiantly, a bare supply of oxygen supporting his words. Hamish wanted all hell to break loose. Chaos. Unleash hell. McEntyre had walked him back towards the Buttery foyer where it was quiet and most importantly out of sight. Almost like a lightning strike, McEntyre smashed his left forearm into the cheekbone of Hamish. There was a clack upon impact. An explosive and quite concussive blow which would knock out most lads cold. Hamish took the full force of the blow and retained a psychotic grin on his face. "Ah now sweetheart, that felt like your sister slapping me."

McEntyre's eye's narrowed to the extent that his pupils became invisible. Rage descended. He sunk a thunderous left jab straight into Hamish's exposed face. "Ah Hey! Ah, now c'mon! That's enough now… piped up Flynn in measly defiance. A defiance which earned him being strong-armed by one of McEntyre's henchmen who wrestled his left hand behind his back and locked an auxiliary choke hold around his neck. Flynn was bent over, rendered immobilized. He looked across as McEntyre held down Hamish and put his knee into his throat. Flynn was shunted alongside Hamish. He felt heavy breathing on the back of his neck as he was locked in position. A violent trigger. The Vestry. The violation. There would be no offer of a biscuit on the way out today. The memories boomed back into this cranium. His father's grave. His mother's promiscuity. His sister's mental heath issues. His inadequacy. The beast in his nature was suddenly laid bare. He felt it rising from the darkness of his soul. He had promised himself things would be different. His first day in Trinity. A suffocating feeling of kill or be killed swept over him. His body began to convulse in the throes of a violent exorcism. Years of hurt morphed into a second being inside him. Blood gushed into his outer capillaries. Detonation of the beast.

"I warned you," he growled. He swung back a hammer fist catching his assailant straight on the temple which knocked him sideways and almost out cold. He turned to face McEntyre and drove a straight left hand into his jaw. He let out a dehumanized roar as he split the penultimate henchman with a rasper of a right hook which landed with a loud clack on the side of his cheek. He looked through the remaining confrère with an even wilder fury. Their eyes briefly met. He looked at Flynn as his fight or flight neurons went into orbit. His flight neurons won the day. He fled like a scalded hound. Hamish picked himself off the floor with a grin as wide as Sydney harbour.

"Well fuck me pink! I won't be calling you Darren again, that's for sure!" McEntyre and the last two of his concussed wolf pack gathered themselves in unison. Flynn arched his shoulders in preparation for further violence. McEntyre shot him a glance of surrender and raised a hand of truce, similar to Roberto Durán vs. Sugar Ray Leonard in 1980, as if to say "No Más!" Flynn's eyes oozed savagery as he glared at McEntyre, "don't ever fuck with me or my friends again." The latter statement brought an ironic laugh from somewhere within the psychological labyrinth of Flynn, he didn't have any friends.

Hamish wiped a trickle of blood from his bottom lip and sparked up a cigarette. He exhaled deeply, "Now Ladies! Enjoy the rest of your evening!" he sneered after them. There was no retort.

Flynn and Hamish retreated to the bar. Hamish looked deep into Flynn's eyes, as if looking to penetrate his soul, "Always the fuckin' quiet ones ye want to watch out for… always the quiet ones, Matey!" He burst out laughing and grabbed two cans from the bar counter, "Cheers, Chuck Norris!" Flynn was still in fight mode and it took a moment for his facial muscles to remember how to smile. *'Who the fuck is this Hamish character?'* he thought to himself, *'am I fuckin' dreaming?'*

A large sinkhole had been blown open deep inside and his inner beast had emerged from the darkest depths. The beast had just made his first public appearance. *'What is happening to me?'* He felt an unworldly nauseousness, as if his entire planet had been moved to a different part of the solar system. Everything around him looked different. Like a hallucinogenic daydream. His eyes opened wider than ever before. They both cracked open another Miller but this time toasted each other with a dull clunk of two cans colliding. The dryness of Flynn's throat was once again irrigated by the bargain-basement warm fizz. Hamish gestured another cigarette towards Flynn who gladly took another Marlboro Light and placed it onto his lips. He inhaled deeply and looked around the room. A new reality dawned at the bottom of this rabbit hole. He had just inflicted physical violence on another person for the first time in his life. And it felt good. *'It felt damn good.'* He ran his left palm along the knuckle of his right hand. For the first time in his life he felt truly alive. His adrenaline rush was accompanied by serotonin bouncing around his organs. He was laid bare to the outside world.

A new lust had been implanted. A lust for chaos, violence and gratification. He looked at Hamish. This felt too surreal. Flynn didn't care whether he was dreaming or not, he just prayed that he didn't wake up any time soon.

Flynn

Chapter Nine: The Swimming Coach and the Spitfire

Hamish looped his head under the buttress to gain sight of the two girls Flynn had procured the Zippo from earlier. "C'mon Flynn," said Hamish, "Let's make friends," as he smoothly arced his way around the corner, fresh can of miller tucked in his right hand. Flynn followed him, thirsty for adventure. In their short time together, Flynn had already come to understand that best practice was to expect the unexpected when it came to Hamish. Hamish and Flynn both presented two quite formidable physical frames as they curved their way back clockwise around the horse shoe structure and towards the two girls. Hamish's cravat was no longer perfectly centred after their earlier quarrel but instead was now knotted almost under his right ear. He still carried himself with a boldness, a bizarre inner autonomy sweeping him along. Hamish momentarily paused and dramatically placed his left hand above his eyeline as if gazing at a distant sunset. The girls were still locked in conversation but you could tell they sensed the almost hypnotic energy of Hamish. Almost commanding a certain cerebral rush with everyone who entered into his psychological domain.

The girl with the Zippo whose name was obviously Sarah, wore black faux leather trousers and a skinny tank top which hugged her modest breasts. She had a long silky neck and narrowed features with short straight hair hanging down to her neckline, almost obscuring her vision on one side. Her black faux leather trousers disappeared seamlessly into black suede over-the-knee boots. Her friend was rounder, blonde and even more voluptuous, carnal voluptuous with an oversized, grey, knitted jumper exposing her left shoulder. She wore bleach-washed blue ripped jeans with the ripped seams on her thighs nicely formulating pockets of lustfulnesses. The jeans were almost able to humanise themselves and extend around her rotund derrière and hug it perfectly. She wore converse which rounded off her rounded sexy casual look perfectly.

Hamish took another thoughtful and deep drag of his cigarette before shifting his shoulders backwards and extending himself to the full boundary of his physical dimension. "Well hello, Ladies… he boomed cordially as he moved towards the two empty seats bordering their table. "We saw you from the bar and thought if we didn't introduce ourselves we might regret it for the rest of our lives." The icebreaker came with a beaming smile and a disarming charisma. They had witnessed the onset of World War III earlier with McEntyre and his confrères but they assumed it must have reached a peaceful conclusion. They still hadn't noticed the swollen and reddening knuckles of Flynn. They were too enchanted by the magnetism of Hamish's opening grandeur.

"My name is Hamish and this is my good friend Daryl." Hamish was a born ring master of ceremonies. His introduction already had a spellbinding effect on their targets of lust. Hamish swooped theatrically into the empty chair. Flynn was on his shoulder. Heretofore, such greetings were a car crash. He would fumble his words, divert his gaze and say something inaudible. The quintessential social reject. Now he took his time and looked both girls directly in the eyes. A world away from the pariah of even a few short minutes ago. Amazing what dishing out of a full force punch in the face can do for a man. The empowerment of watching another man fall beneath his force, watching the knees buckle. The exorcism of fear. Flynn was no longer the whipping boy from the wrong side of the tracks. Suddenly, he realised that money and entitlement were by-products of human life. They could bring status but you couldn't sell or trade status for the current feeling inside his body. Human instinct in the wild plains. In Flynn's case his spirit had been shattered a hundred times over but all those severed pieces had sunk to the bottom of the swamp and moulded into a dormant beast. That beast was now sitting across from two very attractive females with only one thing on his mind.

The charisma of Hamish and the smiling volatility of Flynn made for a formidable team. Flynn drained back his can and exhaled a large plume of smoke. By size alone they cast an intimidating physical presence. Testosterone had already been expended on smashing a few heads. Now the attention turned to carnal satisfaction, the pursuit of the caveman fulfilment.

"I'm Elizabeth, by the way," said the voluptuously rounded blond girl in a middle England accent. She extended her hand towards Flynn with a confident grace, but yet, there was an edge about her. Something deeper inside her smiling demeanour. Flynn could often spot mental fragility in other people. It was his first day in Trinity yet he already felt as if he had a PhD in the nuances of mental anxiety, no matter how subtle and furtive. He sensed a softness inside of Elizabeth, someone who had experienced some sort of mental torment in the past. She had an air of vulnerability. Her friend Sarah was quite the opposite, steely eyed with a strong northern accent. She exuded a toughness and her body language told Flynn that she was battle hardened. A tough nut to crack. He surmised that perhaps the deep conversation had centred around Sarah counselling her stricken friend and hence their tunnel vision when he acquired the earlier light. *'Hamish will be the man to take her down, his charm and charisma could unlock that steel door,'* thought Flynn. He was best served focusing his intention on the softer shoulder of Elizabeth while Hamish could use all his dexterity to gently reel in Sarah, the more robust Marlin. "Daryl, lovely to meet you." Flynn softly took her hand in his and maintained a piercing eye contact, an intense rather than charming seduction. Hamish on the other hand was in 'full monty' mode, bent over on one knee whilst gently administering a kiss to the back of Sarah's knuckles. "Are you for fuckin' real, Darlin?" she barked with her full metal jacket northern Irish accent. She laughed at the same time, deep down she loved it.

Flynn's intuition about their prior counselling session was also on the money. Elizabeth had grown up in the town of Bath in England. She had attended the famous Badminton School in Bristol for her A-Levels and as a contingency had always wanted to go to Bristol University. Two years from her A-Level exams her life began to take a dramatic twist. She had been a champion swimmer throughout her early teens and had even qualified for the World Youth Championships in Los Angeles. She had dreamed big. Swimming at international standard required a grim sacrifice. The punishing training schedule indentured her to three sessions a day, six days a week. Her life became pool, school, weights, gym, home, eat, sleep and repeat. Her life became bereft of fun and teenage frolicking. The years when she should have been finding herself and cultivating relationships were literally spent underwater. The friendships garnered from her early teens soon fell by the wayside as her amateur swimming career became all-consuming. Puberty was coming fast on the horizon and without any other platform for peer interaction, suddenly her swimming coach and mentor became the object of her desires. He was married with two kids. She was one of his most successful protégés. Most of the sessions took place in a team environment but they also had three or four one-on-one sessions a week. It all started innocuously with a simple massage. A tightening of her Achilles and calves. A certain trust developed as she lay prostrate. He soon became enchanted by the touch of her flesh. A synergy developed despite the age gap. A synergy which would bond them together. The ideal affair. The perfect web of deceit. She had no friends that would lift the lid on proceedings. As time went on, confidence grew, and with confidence came familiarity, with familiarity came apathy. He told her he was going on a two-week holiday with his family, *'quality time with his kids.'* On the day of his scheduled return, she was informed whilst warming up in the pool that he had taken a job with the Netherlands high-performance unit. He wasn't coming back. Her hyperventilation at the time seemed excessive, she would have drowned only for the swift actions of one of her teammates. She vomited water from her lungs on the side of the pool, regained consciousness and went home. Her family assumed she would get over his departure after a few days and drive onwards with the new coach in situ. She would never set foot in the pool again.

She became even more insular and completely shut down. She put on weight and developed an eating disorder. Her mind was on the verge of collapse. She was broken-hearted, overweight and now went from a champion swimmer to a nobody. He was gone and he wouldn't be coming back. All the years of sacrifice and dreaming big. The bow and the cradle had crash-landed like the Space Shuttle Challenger. Eventually she began to plateau and developed a foothold of equilibrium. Her grades steadied but she never resumed training again. Her single-minded pursuit of international swimming excellence had left her alone and isolated. She became a boarder in school which left her even more exposed. She never confided in anyone about her past. As if she had taken a vow of omertà. Her suffering in silence was misconstrued by her classmates but also gave the bullies carte blanche to torment her. A growing darkness enveloped her thoughts. She envisaged ending it all. Something inside her managed to launch a final rearguard action. She finally sought advice from her family doctor and was prescribed anxiety medication. Xanax and Valium became her best friend. She finally broke down and confided in her Mum three months before the A-Levels that she was bullied but still the great mystery of her psychological collapse remained unspoken. It was agreed that she would go abroad to study. "Hang in there." Each day became one day closer to liberation. The thoughts of never seeing the faces or places in Bristol ever again motivated her to keep on going. There was light at the end of tunnel. She held her own in the A-Levels and got enough points for English and Italian in Trinity College. A fresh start. This would never happen to her again. When her flight took off from Bristol Airport she looked downwards just before disappearing into the clouds. She allowed herself a smile. She was going to find herself.

Sarah on the other hand was carved from pure Belfast blood, sweat and tears. The generations before her had laboured hard in the flourishing linen and shipbuilding industries of the Belfast docklands. She was from Catholic stock and there were no shortcuts coming from a family of labourers. Her father, Gerry, despite being understated and quiet in demeanour had acquired small sites upon which he built his empire. They had invested down south in strategic property portfolios and when the Good Friday Agreement kicked in and trade agreements began to accelerate they were well-placed. In particular residential and commercial holdings in Dublin were bearing serious fruit.

Sarah's mother, Sal, was a tough woman, she originally hailed from The Falls Road in Belfast. Sal's family were staunch republicans, many of whom served in the IRA. Her father was arrested for paramilitary activities and served time in the Maze prison at Long Kesh. Her childhood was volatile at best. Never really knowing when somebody close would be taken away. Republicanism represented mixed ideals for her. She grew up with the songs, violence and impassioned rhetoric. She realised very early in life that as tough and unyielding as the Catholic Republican movement was, the Protestant unionist movement could match them every step of the way. There would be no take over, nor would there be any surrender for either side. The Irish and UK governments would support a peace process but any ideals of a united Ireland and the displacement of either religion was fictional in the extreme. She gradually grew hardened to the environment and over time even more agnostic to the ideals that Catholics would take over and claim what was rightfully theirs. Every bombing and shooting lead to more deaths, more bloodshed and more people taken away. She met Sarah's father, Gerry, in White's Tavern thirty years previously. He was different. She could hardly remember him saying a word the first time they met. Perhaps he was the counterweight of the volatility and political violence of The Falls Road. He hardly ever spoke of hatred and Catholic oppression. He was a grafter, had opened up his first small premises in the docks and employed two men. He steadily acquired more property and began to build a business. They married five years after their first meeting in Whites. It was shortly before their marriage that Sal realised that Gerry's father had been fatally wounded in the Bogside massacre, Bloody Sunday 1972. He had never spoken of it.

Gerry had grown up without a father. The assumption was a scorned child would seek revenge and only the infliction of death and destruction would be enough to mourn his passing. Gerry, however, grew up with a quiet sadness. He had been approached by many republican leaders over the years about joining their movement but he respectfully declined. He was a victim of the Troubles, his Dad was dead and there was no bringing him back. He decided he wanted to build a future where his own son and daughter wouldn't have to stand by his graveside with men in balaclavas firing their guns in the air. To achieve this there would be no shortcuts. He embodied humility. Even when money came along it never changed his work ethic. Both himself and Sal shared the same values. Neither took anything for granted and instilled that ethos in their children. They espoused the virtue that people themselves were greater than religion. The Northern Irish conflict had broken Gerry and Sal in so many ways but they were a success story amongst the chaos. They were both so single-minded and their mental fortitude was passed down to their children. Sarah now studying in Trinity and John Paul studying in Cambridge. One of their properties was a luxurious sixth floor apartment in Charlotte

Quay which they reluctantly decided would be an ideal base for Sarah during her tenure in Trinity College, however long that may last.

Both Sarah and Elizabeth were sipping down Bacardi or just Cokes as far as the bar staff were concerned. The perk of the female student. Topping up your drinks in a darkened corner of a student bar with your Bacardi. Sarah's eagle eye spied swelling around Flynn's hand. "That's some right knuckle you have there sweetie, have you been a bold boy?" she enquired with a devilish grin. Hamish interjected, "This is my Guardian Angel!" as he leaned across, sparking laughter from all four of them. "So you can look after yourself then?" said Elizabeth with a smile as the laughter subsided. "Sometimes," said Flynn as he ran his fingers over his swollen knuckle, "only when the occasion demands it though, I want to make sure I can protect my friends." He shot a smile in Hamish's direction and returned his gaze back to Elizabeth, "so do you think you need a Bodyguard?" his eyes engaging hers and penetrating her guard. She smiled and diverted her gaze, Morse code for *'Oh yes I most certainly do, I want you guarding my naked body after a few more Bacardis.'* Her actual response was: "Do I really look like I need a bodyguard, Daryl?" with a lingering smile. Elizabeth was getting into the spirit of it, the Bacardis were kicking in and she still had powerful shoulders from the years of elite training. She pulled up her sleeve and seductively tensed her bicep. "Impressive," said Flynn, "maybe it's you that should be my bodyguard." All four of them laughed.

Flynn kept eye contact with Elizabeth. He had her on the ropes, he had penetrated her guard. Hamish was loving every second. His most unlikely wingman had not only saved his bacon in a bar fight but was now stepping up to the plate as Michael Cassio with the females. Hamish may have parachuted them behind enemy lines, but Flynn was turning out to be just as formidable in the territorial battle. Hamish could now focus his time on procuring the affections of Sarah.

"So, what do you do here in Trinity when you're not beating people up, Daryl?" asked Elizabeth. "Chat to beautiful women," responded Flynn with even greater confidence. The world was suddenly his oyster, he felt as though blood was pumping through his every capillary faster than ever before. "But when I'm not chatting to beautiful women, I'm studying History and Philosophy." Flynn suddenly had a way about him. He didn't have the explosive magnetism of Hamish but he had an intrigue, a powerful vulnerability which commanded a similar gravitation towards him. "And what made ye choose those subjects, Daryl? If ye don't mind me asking?" asked Sarah with intrigue. "My life," said Flynn, he smiled and took a long gulp of his can. The four of them laughed with renewed vigour, a natural synergy was developing. Hamish leapt to his feet as if he'd been struck by lightning. "Aye, Aye Tigers! I think I know what time it is! It's that magical time of day when we all need a few Sambucas to stimulate our sensory organs!"

Before the protestations could even commence, he disappeared to the bar. The three of them were left in momentary silence. "So, where are you from, Daryl?" asked Elizabeth. "I'm from a very beautiful part of Dublin called Artane, a great spot for a safari but only if you're willing to see the animals from a distance," he chuckled as he finished his quip and savoured another warm gulp of Miller. "Ah so you're what they call a

Northsider then?" fired back Sarah with her northern wit, "did ye have to steal a car to get here today?" They all bellowed out laughter and lit up a cigarette. She continued, "Ye see, the great thing about this place is nobody gives a fuck where you're from as long as you're crazy enough. My family are originally from the toughest side of Catholic Belfast, but if that handsome Protestant Fucker wanted to fuck my brains out I'd wrap my legs around him all night long!" She had a way with words. The insane charisma of the Nordies. Flynn barked out a deep laugh. He looked at Elizabeth. He wouldn't mind her legs wrapped around him all night long. A roar went up from behind Flynn, "did somebody say *'handsome Protestant Fucker'*?" Hold on to your hats you crazy cats because Daddy is coming home!" Hamish dramatically swung a tray into the middle of the table containing eight shots of Sambuca. "Wooooooooooooh! Viva la revolución!" he cried and set ablaze to each glass. The awesome sight of the blue velvet Sambuca flame was quite enchanting. The smell of burning liquorice and coffee beans. The Italian originators from over one hundred years ago, and long dead in their graves, must have rolled with pride that their elderberry creation had evolved into the stunt devil shot of the kamikaze student.

"Right now ladies, these will put hair on your chest!" bellowed Hamish as he resumed his seat with renewed vigour, "one tip and one tip only, don't forget to blow the fuckin' thing out and lick your glass before consumption." The four of them raised their shots. "So, what are we toasting?" asked Sarah, her eyes beaming with excitement. "Here's to our sex lives!" piped up Hamish. "Let's toast great sex, great friendships and beautiful lives thereafter. And most of all Protestants fuckin'g Catholics or do I have that the wrong way around?" he shoved Sarah and broke into psychotic laughter. His laughter was both infectious and disarming. Nobody around the table cared about religion, politics or wealth. They were four students liberated and getting to know each other. Two shots of Sambuca each were a great severance of the senses. Like the formal cutting of the umbilical cord of sobriety.

The euphoria of the moment was only briefly interrupted by Flynn feeling an overwhelming pain in his sides around his kidneys and bladder. The madness, insanity and emotional rollercoaster had somehow imbued him with an amnesia to relieve himself. "Won't be long," he uttered as he scraped his way up off the table and began weaving his way along the tiled floor. The kitchens had been on full blast and the walls were starting to sweat. Condensation formed a thick film on the hall down to the toilets. Flynn ran his left hand along the wall and gathered a pocket of moisture on his index finger. That touch was important, as the cold sensation proved that he wasn't dreaming. *'Imagine waking up after all this and realising nothing lay ahead. Waking up in that shitty room, making stand-offish small talk with his mother and sister before facing the world. Fuck that world.'* He was sick of the real world. The old Flynn-world could burn in hell. This was a fantasy land and now he got a taste for acceptance he wanted to see how deeply the rabbit hole really went. He crossed the threshold of the toilets and smelled that beautiful "freshers" week aroma of vomit and shite. He was burning oil at this stage and had about three seconds to undo his zip before disaster. There was a cacophony of retching from the cubicle next to him. He could hear the hollow burn of someone's throat as they relieved the contents of their stomach of some poison. There was also an overpowering smell of shite, the sort that would emanate freshly from someone who obviously overdosed their intestines and was now exploding like a Luftwaffe Messerschmitt. The perpetrator was either unconscious or in a state of serenity. Poor sick boy in the cubicle next to him retched uncontrollably. Every few seconds the jolt from his latest vomit would catapult him against the door as if he was being devoured by a tiger. Flynn was frozen in time, however, he arched his back and used his left palm to balance himself against the wall. He let out a gentle exhalation. That quasi-orgasmic feeling of the emptying of an overloaded bladder. Sick boy sounded like he had finally hit the bottom of this stomach, no doubt the last remnants of his bile had made landfall and now the dry retching commenced. Flynn could sense by the violent and sporadic sound effects that it would be a miracle for even forty percent of his vomit to nestle inside the toilet bowl. No doubt the rim, floors and walls were now nicely decorated. Flynn heard one big flush, fidgeting with the lock, closely followed by the miracle of sick boy emerging from the cubicle like a scurvy ridden sailor. He stumbled across to the wash basin, cupped some water onto his face and stumbled back out the door into the battlefield. The destruction of the toilet being his mini legacy. Flynn was now finally at the drip stage, as he exhaled a further sigh of euphoria.

At that moment, there was movement in the second cubicle. Luftwaffe Messerschmitt man was obviously starting to come around. Flynn heard the crackle of toilet paper. *'Best off to clear the decks before that animal re-engaged with the world.'* He was on tenterhooks, and the last thing he wanted was any engagement with the originator of that nuclear stench.

Flynn

Flynn headed back to the jungle, the temporary hiatus from the madness had not broken his will to embrace the chaos. He departed the Buttery toilet and left Luftwaffe Spitfire Shite man to fend for himself. He walked towards the throng of noise, the zoo of drunken Freshers. He was part of it, no longer the freak lingering in the shadows. Nobody around here knew his background. He embraced the drunken haze, let it all wash over him as he carried on. He walked through the doors and back into the mayhem, like a boxer making a ring entrance, he walked into the Coliseum of Iniquity. He felt empowered. Almost invincible. Almost. There was a chink of doubt somewhere inside him still screaming out for validation of this new universe. *'Nonsense'* he thought to himself, he had felt every sinew of physical and emotional catharsis over the last few hours. *'Of course I'm not dreaming, please don't tell me I'm fuckin' dreaming?'* Flynn was stopped dead in his tracks. The sight of an empty table turned his stomach upside down. He double-checked the location. Yes, indeed, it was the same table underneath the buttress where himself, Hamish, Sarah and Elizabeth had just been. Another two Freshers breezed past him and sidled up to their girlfriends in the same spot. His heart sank.

'Have I imagined this whole fuckin' thing?' The stress alone made him physically recoil. His heart was gripped by palpitations. *'Could this beautiful experience be demolished? 'Have I lost my fuckin' mind? Have I really invented all this?'* The invincibility drained from his pores as he collapsed against the arch of a buttress. He raised his hands to his face, as if to cover the torment in store. He was almost about to slump on the ground when he caught the scent of a familiar perfume followed by the call of a familiar voice, "Daryl I have your jacket, are you OK? We're waiting for you in the foyer."

It was Elizabeth. She leaned over and put an arm around him. Flynn felt a kaleidoscope of emotions as he felt her affection. He felt his swollen right knuckles as he ran his fingers through his hair. *'Back in the fuckin' game! It is real after all.'* He gripped his right knuckle with his left hand to further corroborate his reality. "Are you OK, Daryl?" Elizabeth asked again. "Can I tell ye a secret, Elizabeth? I've never felt better in my whole life than I do at this very moment." The invincibility came flooding back into his capillaries. "Would you mind if I… ?" Flynn leaned across and kissed her.

Her moist lips acquiesced to his. He held her close and explored every sinew of her tonsils. The perfect embrace. He ran his hands over her muscular back muscles. A moment ago he felt as if he was dreaming, now he was living the dream. Elizabeth caressed the back of his neck and ran her fingernails down his spine, the superficial incision arousing his senses. Her carnal voluptuousness was now in his hands. "That feels so nice," said Flynn, Elizabeth opened her eyes and ran her hand along his cheek, her eyes squinted with mutual arousal, "I love the way you kiss me." The intensity of Flynn's kiss made her tremble. It wasn't even so much his technique as the adrenaline coursing through his veins, the transfer of energy, the feeling of warmth. Hamish and Sarah admired their loving embrace from the foyer, Hamish wrapped his muscular forearms around Sarah's chest. "Ye can't beat a good wingman to show you the way!" said Hamish as he sparked them both into laughter. "Now where were we? Those lips are just crying out for mine." He pulled Sarah in close and locked her lips for another few moments.

Flynn

Chapter Ten: Smiley Faced Balloon

Elizabeth and Flynn simultaneously came up for air, a film of moisture circumnavigated their lips. The tactility of a drunken kiss arousing their senses even further. "I do hope you're enjoying the taste of Sambuca just as much as me," Elizabeth giggled and pulled Flynn closer as she placed her head on his chest. She felt his warmth and his heart beating beneath his t-shirt. A certain comfort and security swept over her. "Well come on you lot," bellowed Hamish with a charismatic grin as he pulled a large drag from his cigarette. "What's the plan, me man?" enquired Flynn as they weaved their way out the door. Elizabeth interlocked their fingers. Flynn could not remember ever holding hands with a girl in public, but now it felt so natural. He never held Rachel's hand. Even when they were alone he would walk beside her, a good yard apart. His affections were always limited to the business end of climaxing. This had been an afternoon like no other and its trajectory was only going one way! "We're all going back to mine for a Freshers welcome party!" Hamish flashed him a psychotic smile. The sort of smile that says *this is worth your while, Matey.* Flynn felt liberated as he burst out into the twilight of Front Square hand in hand with Elizabeth. A casual hook-up but to him it was symbolic. He had crossed the Rubicon. He no longer felt constrained by his tortuous past. He smiled to himself as he looked towards the relative tranquillity of the front arch. The stands now lay unmanned and dormant for the night. There was no intimidating gauntlet. The Daryl Flynn who walked through that arch was also dead. His nerves, anxiety and low resolution had died with him. He gripped Elizabeth's hand even tighter and swept a lustful glance in her direction.

'Thank fuck that bastard is dead,' he surmised. *'There's a new sheriff in town and he's going to make up for lost time, a lot of fuckin' lost time.'* He pulled Elizabeth even closer for a warm embrace and kiss. He felt the cobble lock beneath his feet, the same cobble lock that, earlier, had dismantled Daryl Flynn.

The four of them walked past the tennis courts and towards Botany Bay dorms. A few abstemious tennis revellers still pelted balls across the net oblivious to the memo that the only raison d'être for being on campus was to get pole-axed drunk. "Fuckin' Idiots!" roared Hamish as he trundled by hand in hand with Sarah. A couple of scowls were fired back from the tennis court, but no dialogue, they knew better than to engage some crazed Fresher full of diesel. *'What sort of moronic creatures played tennis on an evening like this when there were so many other pursuits on offer?'* The light was fading fast as they entered the sanctuary of the dorms.

"Are you sure about this?" Elizabeth looked into Flynn's eyes as she held the LSD cookie on the palm of her hand. Flynn, a rookie and novice when it came to drugs, was suddenly being asked his expert opinion. The fight neurons inside Flynn's brain were still celebrating victory from the earlier 'kill or be killed' showdown with McEntyre and his Cronies. He had not only crossed bridges but blown them up since his earlier whimper through the front arch. Now was not the time to take a backward step. "Sure jaysus it's all the rage, let's give it a lash!" He kissed her, a deep and passionate tonsil caresser. He recoiled slightly and without hesitation swallowed his own acid tab in one go. "Destination unknown!" said Elizabeth as she followed suit. Hamish and Sarah had already ingested theirs several minutes earlier and were in the process of french-kissing on the couch. Flynn looked across at them but this time he didn't see Hamish and Sarah. They had been replaced by two Saint Bernard dogs, slobbering all over each other as drool oozed onto the couch below. Flynn erupted into laughter. He looked back towards Elizabeth who now morphed into a smiley-faced happy balloon. He pulled her close. The tactility of her kiss and feel transcended everything that had gone before. Together they floated into the bedroom. Flynn began to undress Elizabeth, it felt like a full foliation of her individual layers of skin. Each layer gave him an enhanced arousal. Elizabeth reciprocated every feel, every engagement of seduction. Flynn felt her nails glide down his bare chest as his jeans seemed to float downwards towards the floor. He felt his boxer shorts tumbling over his hips. The ultimate catharsis which would render him naked. He felt all the blood inside his body drain into his penis, his heart fluttered wildly as his blood pressure blasted into orbit. It felt as if his penis was the only answer to extricate himself of the pressure cooker building inside his body.

"You look amazing," said Elizabeth. "So do you," replied Flynn as they interchanged more *oohs, aahs and yeses*. The only thing on his mind was penetrating this "smiley faced happy balloon". He finally felt himself inside her, the feel of her moist vaginal balloon accelerated his sensation. Contraception was overlooked in lieu of the drug-induced mayhem. Flynn, a giant happy balloon himself made love to his fellow 'psycho-naut'. Two smiley-faced happy balloons bringing each other to climax. Flynn detected a shrill trembling from his fellow balloonist which drove him further towards climax.

Suddenly he felt like he was about to explode. Every sinew of skin, flesh and bone seemed to gather around his love organ. He screamed like Tarzan as his love balloon burst. An orgasm which felt like the docking of the Hindenburg, a fireball of pleasure reverberated around his body. The power of the orgasm suffocated him to the extent that he felt like passing out. He collapsed on top of his fellow balloonist. Her touch and nudity maintained his pleasure island of tactility.

Hamish had produced a bottle of red wine as his role as host. A cheap South African Cabernet Sauvignon number. However, to students and particularly freshers, red wine was still red wine, a preserved commodity for the great and the good. After the distribution of tabs he settled down on the couch with Sarah. She didn't disguise her lust for him. It wasn't their first rodeo when it came to recreational drugs. Unlike Flynn and Elizabeth there would be no procrastination. Once settled, she crossed both her forearms in an X and slid her top halfway up her abdomen, enough for Hamish to see her moist and perfectly rippled chassis. Hamish's arousal hit fever pitch, his eyes narrowed as he wrapped both hands around her exposed lower back and pulled her close. Sarah pressed her lips up to his ear and gently whispered, "Now I want you to fuck my brains out." The time for talking was over. He led her to a bedroom across the hall. Once the door closed behind them, it all kicked off. Hyper passion. Hyper arousal. Sarah ripped open Hamish's silk shirt buttons and ran her fingers up his chest onto his shoulder blades and peeled back the rest of his shirt, exposing his bare, chiselled beauty beneath. His sodden silk shirt stuck momentarily to his biceps as she undressed him. Once bare-chested, he pulled her close to him and seamlessly lifted her soaking top over her head. He kissed her deeply and undid her black-laced bra-strap and let it gently fall to the floor. With the top half of their bodies laid bare, they embraced. The magical first skin on skin contact, accelerating arousal. A deep, prolonged embrace punctuated by kisses until Hamish lowered her back on the bed. He buried deep kisses on her neck before satisfying each nipple and running his tongue down her abdomen. He slid down her faux black leather pants and exposed her perfectly toned legs. Her sex laid bare and inviting. He unbuckled his belt and stood upright to accentuate the depth of his arousal. No more words were required. Telepathy took over, both their bodies wanted each other with ravenous lust. This would be a long night ahead. The best was yet to come.

Flynn

Chapter Eleven: The Morning After

Flynn woke up to the sensation of foreign bedsheets gripping his perspiring body. The first few seconds of paradise. Still unaware of his surroundings. His brain still hadn't calibrated the madness of the night before. It is often said that the first few seconds of transition from sleep to consciousness are the happiest. Within those seconds, the brain has not yet engaged any emotional interaction. Those few seconds when we are truly liberated before the conscious takes over and we must face our daily demons all over again. Flynn felt the warmth of another naked body beside him as his brain went into overdrive. *'Where the fuck am I and what the fuck had happened last night?'* His brain began to frantically search for answers. Flynn, the memory man, was suddenly facing a blank data bank. The re-loading of his brain's hard drive was immediately interrupted when the naked body beside him rolled over to embrace him, subconsciously the innate human requirement for carnal warmth became overpowering. He reciprocated as he felt the warm voluptuous blond body beside him, the smell of her long blond hair and stale perfume. Adam and Eve. Their genitalia naked and exposed. Flynn, at first, felt like Flynn until the Hoover Dam in his brain burst and all the emotions came flooding back. His heart was pounding in overdrive, his bloodstream still pumping with enough narcotics and alcohol to last him till at least evening time. His head ached from dehydration, as if an Indian tomahawk had penetrated his skull and severed the nerve endings in his brain. "Holy Jaysus, what a night," as he held Elizabeth in a giant lustful bear hug triggering a chemical reaction inside his body. His love hormones drained into his penis as he prepared for more.

Flynn

Flynn climbed on top of Elizabeth, a warm duvet on his back and a warm voluptuous body beneath him. He felt more erect than ever before in his life, his heart pounded at the impending penetration. Her slightly moist thighs parted and acceded to his lustful advance. She ran her fingers up Flynn's muscular biceps and around his shoulder blades and glided her nails seductively down his back. His body descended between the beautiful chasm created by the detachment of her legs. She pulled up and anchored her knees slightly upwards to make the landing strip even broader. Flynn felt the initial resistance of her clitoris. His erection easily bypassed this and slowly penetrated, the warm moist walls of her vagina enveloped his penis as Elizabeth exhaled with euphoric pain. The sort of beautiful pain that leads to stimulation of the senses. The curvature of her warm vaginal walls made Flynn even more aroused and erect. He positioned both hands around her perfectly formed bottom which tightened upon touch and became even more perfect, he leaned in and kissed her, feeling his body against her warm breasts which flexed and stimulated upon impact. They both breathed heavily as he increased the rhythm of each thrust. "That feels so fuckin' nice," she uttered with elongated pronunciation. She ran her nails down his back and onto his bum to metronomically control the rhythm of their intercourse. "This is the best feeling in the world," said Flynn, his muscles tensing and feeling greater empowerment with each thrust. The blood vessels in his neck enlarging with the increased physicality and pursuit of pleasure. A film of perspiration coated them both in perfect symmetry. She increased her sighs of pleasure. Gradually, the sensory interaction built more and more stimulation as her vaginal walls began to flood in preparation for climax. She shuddered violently and scraped her nails into Flynn's back. Lift-off at Cape Canaveral. Full rocket boosters. Flynn felt the greater lubrication deep in her love passage, the signal for him to increase his thrusts, deeper and more purposeful as he steered her closer and closer to climax. Defying the laws of gravity, Elizabeth appeared to levitate on the bed as she exhaled a battle cry of pleasure before slumping breathlessly on the flat of her back. Flynn wasn't finished. He could already feel himself on the precipice of climax. And better again that golden moment where the man has already pleasured his opposite number as she lies satisfied and exhausted beneath him. He's now left with an open goal, a penalty kick. *'The world is your oyster, Flynn,'* he tells himself as he thrusts deeply for all he's worth. "Come on! Oh, Daryl yes! Give it to me! Yesss," she groans some more and wraps her arms around Flynn's back, guiding each pleasurable thrust. Flynn barks out a loud screech. He's in the departure lounge of the orgasmic terminal. A few seconds later, he grunts and wrestles Elizabeth into the strongest bear hug known to mankind. The catharsis of love insemination. His body transitions from one-hundred-miles-an-hour-thrusts to a state of quasi -epileptic shock as his body goes into that sensual paralysis upon climax. He slumps his full weight on top of Elizabeth. Even though he constricts her breathing she still soothes his back as he extricates every last drop of his love. Their bodies bound in perfect unison, both climaxed and happy.

Flynn's muscles quiver as he reaches for the box of cigarettes and lighter on the bedside locker. He stretches across with dexterity, careful not to dislodge himself from his perfect pose of insertion inside Elizabeth. They both breath heavily, a mixture of physical exertion and psychological utopia. Last thing Flynn needs is as cigarette but it's the first thing he wants. He emits a satisfied groan and breaks into a smile. He regains his perfect equilibrium on top of Elizabeth. He slowly grants his erection the autonomy to drain itself in harmonious surrounds. The next few moments are just as pleasurable. Fait accompli. A sensual film of perspiration clings to the bottom of Elizabeth's neck, a fusion of both their efforts. The sort of emission where the human body has experienced the four horsemen of the apocalypse; conquest, war, famine and death. His conquest lay naked beneath him, he had his war the night before with McEntyre and his goons, his famine he had endured for as long as he could remember and his death was his father, or perhaps something more imminent. Flynn kissed Elizabeth, the perfect irrigation for his Saharan tonsils before a post sex cigarette. He gently began to retract from her honey pot.

'All good things must come to an end, Flynn.' He slid his giant frame onto his left shoulder and relinquished their full court suffocating synergy. Flynn lay on the flat of his back as Elizabeth snuggled her head on his chest and wrapped her left arm and left leg around his body. They both craved love, and the warmth from sexual desire. Flynn took out two Marlboro lights and threw the packet back on the bedside locker. "Holy Jaysus! What a night!" He gently placed a cigarette between Elizabeth's lips and sparked up her cigarette before repeating the same trick on himself. His lips were chapped from all the festivities so the cigarette found an easy bearing between a few crevasses. He took the first drag deep into his lungs. The lack of food and hydrating fluids allowed each outlier of nicotine to pollinate the innermost alveoli of his lungs and send a dizziness back up his oesophagus and into his membranes. He lay back and enjoyed the buzz. Light-headed dizziness wrapped up beside a naked woman. The light on the ceiling danced merrily away. Life was beautiful.

Flynn

Flynn took a brief scan and recce of the room. He seemed to recall the room as being entirely different the night before. "Ah Holy Jaysus! I'm in some hula-hoop here this morning." He exhaled another long plume of smoke towards the ceiling and cuddled Elizabeth even closer. The hangover from drink and drugs added another layer of tactility to his outer skin. Every touch and feel became accentuated. His brain power was very much limited to the *now*. He previously read an article on the art of mindfulness, how to live in the present. Right now, this was not a problem. *'I remember fuck-all from last night,'* he thought to himself, his mind began to rewind the blank cassette through every millisecond hoping to find some items but uncovering a blank canvas. Flynn ventured forward, "I remembered these dorm rooms being a lot more antiquated last night!" unsure of himself even as he said it. Elizabeth bellowed out laughter as she exhaled and rolled on top of Flynn for a kiss. "You're not in Trinity dorms now Daryl, you're in my room! This is Charlotte Quay!" She laughed as she lay back again. "You'll probably be wondering why your clothes over there are also soaking wet? Do you remember the boats last night? We nearly drowned." A flush of perspiration bolted into Flynn's temples. "Ah good Lord Jaysus, don't be telling me that first thing!" Flynn gestured towards his temple. "At least give the hamster in here a chance to get running on his little wheel." Elizabeth rolled back with laughter. "Well at least the big hamster down here is working well." She slid her hand down his chiselled abdomen. "Mmmm, that feels nice!" said Flynn. He lay back on the pillow as Elizabeth pleasured him. Every touch reverberated deep into his pleasure chamber. He lay with both arms back in crucifixion pose, opening up his body to every arousing stimulation. He reached yet another climax. The love potion was now fully drained from his limbs. He reached across and sparked up another cigarette. "So tell me about these boats." Elizabeth cradled her head on his chest. The elevated yet perfect rhythm of his heart and lungs undulated beneath her. Flynn placed a cigarette in her mouth and carefully sparked her up. "The age of chivalry is far from dead," he said with a smile, "now fill in a few gaps for me?" Elizabeth giggled. "Okay, so let's start at the beginning, so what's the last thing you remember?" Flynn knew she was playing him to an extent but was happy to oblige, tucked under the covers with her voluptuous naked body he could be playing *I spy with my little eye* and still be happy. His memory loss didn't adversely worry him as he was getting rapid flashbacks as the seconds rolled by. "Okay, so here's what I know." He exhaled as if he was about to impart some age-old wisdom. "Okay, so after we popped the LSD I remember making love to a giant smiley faced happy balloon." This was immediately interrupted by Elizabeth who shot him a short elbow to the ribs. "Oi, keep that up and there will be more where that came from!" She laughed and lay back on his chest again. "Then I remember we went out somewhere, somewhere with purple fluorescent light… and fuckin' hell, I remember there being a giant bison hanging on the wall! I think we may have had another altercation of some sorts and then yes I do vaguely remember falling in the water somewhere. Jaysus, last time I was on a boat was down in Arklow when I was ten and that was a bleedin' pedalo!" He inhaled deeply on this cigarette as he focused on a spot on the ceiling in perfect pensive thought. "I'm only bluffing, Daryl, I was off my tits as well. I do remember you threatening to kill some guys from the Hockey club and then robbing a boat, thereafter I'm hazy enough myself."

Flynn

Chapter 12: What Actually happened

The purple lights were mesmerising in Judge Roy Beans. Crazy décor, in particular the stuffed Buffalo Bison Head which hung on the wall and accentuated the hallucinogenic rampage of the four confrères. Every few minutes Flynn would look up at the Bison and break into laughter or simply stare pensively at this taxidermist masterpiece. They had commandeered the famous window seats which gave them a Bird's-eye view of every passer-by on Nassau street. Flynn was being swept along in an emotional rollercoaster. He leaned in and kissed Elizabeth before his attention switched back to the giant bison on the wall. Perspiration flowed steadily down this brow; his t-shirt was becoming saturated. His attention would then quickly shift to a passer-by; "Look at the bleedin' head on yer man!" and after a few seconds more his curiosity would then be spiked by the frivolous sight of someone carrying a shopping bag, "Jaysus yer one is some size of a unit, a pudding." He inhabited his own little world. He turned back to kiss Elizabeth and pulled her close for another elongated passionate kiss. He tried to keep his eyes open but he knew the giant Buffalo Bison head was hanging on the wall looking at him. He moved Elizabeth around to face the opposite direction. "Is that big bastard hanging on the wall still looking at us?" he asked, Elizabeth looked up and broke into a fit of giggles. "I think he likes you, Daryl." They both broke into laughter but a couple of minutes later Flynn was eyeing him up again.

Hamish and Sarah were dancing wildly at the table beside them. Their wild dance routine was only punctuated by the odd water break for Bacardi and coke. Hamish and Flynn made eye contact and both started roaring and laughing uncontrollably. "Flynn you fuckin' giant can of piss! You're the greatest thing since sliced bread mate!"

The laughter continued without any trigger. Both girls joined the bandwagon of infectious laughter. Hamish tried to slump back on his stool but missed it entirely and sprawled out on the ground. This propagated another tsunami of laughter. Flynn hyperventilated as his chest tightened, he gasped for air as the laughter consumed his whole body. Saliva burst the banks of his lower lip as drool cascaded towards the floor. Through his LSD-induced eyes, Hamish metamorphosed into an orangutan rolling around the floor. Every time Hamish laughed Flynn saw the gaping mouth of a great red Ape. Flynn convulsed with screeching laughter. A screech which could even be heard over the rocking music. Half the bar turned to see where the unworldly jungle sound was emanating. The higher Flynn's pitched laugh became, the more Hamish, Sarah and Elizabeth crippled themselves with laughter. Flynn felt his temperature skyrocket, he felt like a furnace inside him was melting the walls of his skin. He was parched. He downed the Bacardi and coke, but his tonsils still felt like a dust bowl. He headed for the toilet, he had to get water and douse the flames on his skin. The hallucinogenic surrounds created an even more bamboozling effect on the senses. As he passed by the bar, he noticed two aliens drinking cocktails. Their slimy green skin and wrinkled faces freaked him out further. They both stared at him with their giant bug-eyes bulging out from their eye sockets. They grinned. A goading "fuck you, Flynn" type of alien grin. He had no time for combat, priority was to get to the toilet. He would deal with the aliens on his way back. The two aliens were none other than Nick Brewster and Charlie Stokes, stalwarts and part of the high Chaparral of the Trinity Hockey Club. They were "made men". Blazer men in hockey circles. Both from big money, good schools and most importantly; part of the inner golden circle of Trinity College. Flynn was oblivious to their identity and standing. At that very moment, they were both highly irrelevant. His only priority was to extinguish the rising flames which had broken out all over his body. His pace quickened as he charged towards the toilets. He barrelled through the door and finally reached the oasis of the handwash basin, whereupon he frantically splashed water on his face and body. His ears were on fire, they were the lightning rods for the inferno. A Nigerian toilet attendant tasked with selling aftershave and deodorant to a generally civilised customer base was now confronted by this maniac splashing water all over his enclave. "Hey man! What the hell are you doing?" he roared. Flynn was undeterred. Every splash of water gave him partial relief. He stood at the sink splashing water with both hands. Then cupped more water and began drinking it. "Ah hey Brother, don't drink that my man! That is bad water! What the hell you doing?" Flynn recoiled and gave him a look. The sort of look that intimated violence if he uttered another word. The LSD gave him a ferocious, bloodshot look. The devil incarnate.

Flynn burst his way back through the door, intent on finding the cocktail drinking aliens at the bar, both of whom were still there and in perfect poise. Both Brewster and Stokes saw the mad man coming but assumed he was making a beeline back towards the door when suddenly and without warning he made a lunge for them. Before they knew it, Flynn had gripped them both around the throat. All Flynn could make out was these alien eyes staring back at him as he tried to increase the pressure on their asphyxiation. Pandemonium ensued as Brewster and Stokes' entourage leapt on top of Flynn to defend their beloved "made-men". Hamish then ran and fired himself like a human cannonball into the mix as bodies lay strewn on the ground. All Flynn saw was a flying orangutan making mince meat of a few adversaries. A couple of bouncers finally waded into the melee and began separating bodies, unsure of who were the cowboys and who were the Indians. Both Sarah and Elizabeth were on hand to try and coax their men away. Flynn got back to his feet as Elizabeth tugged at his sleeve to get out of there. "Just one last thing before we go, Princess," Flynn bent over and gave her a kiss before sprinting back towards their table. He took a run and jump which catapulted him towards the wall. He grabbed onto the horns of the giant Buffalo Bison head and suddenly dangled in midair. The bouncers now realised the identity of the perpetrator and gave chase.

Even the toilet attendant had joined the fray to identify Flynn as the agent provocateur. Flynn wrapped his legs around the Bison and temporarily suspended himself beyond their grasp. However, a couple of bolts began to give way. The giant hairy structure and Flynn were now at the mercy of gravity. One of the bouncers caught Flynn by his trouser leg and attempted to pull him downwards. In doing so, he brought down the house of cards. The impact was surreal, almost cinematic. Flynn still gripped the Buffalo Bison head. He smiled, oblivious to the unconscious bouncer beneath him. The other bouncer made a go for Flynn but Hamish blocked his path and ended up being wrestled to the ground himself. The brief commotion allowed Sarah and Elizabeth to get Flynn back to his feet. "Come on, Daryl, we better get you out of here," roared Sarah. Flynn followed them as they made their way to the door. Hamish bolted his grip on the bouncer who now lost patience and rained punches down on top of him. Hamish let go under the force of a few bad smacks. He lay dazed and prone and readied himself for a knockout blow. Suddenly there was a thundering clack as the bouncers body crumbled across him. It was Flynn. "I think it's time we all got the fuck out of here!" Hamish flashed him a giant grin despite blood dripping from his nose. They limped out the door but got into their stride as they ran down Nassau. Flynn could feel the air rush through his lungs as they ran at full throttle, it was if they were paragliding over the mountains. They whooped and hollered. "Viva la revolución!"

The four revolutionaries bounded over the bridge and descended into Charlotte Quay. The coronation of their invincibility well and truly rubber-stamped. They already tasted plenty of blood but were still in the mood for one last fandango of havoc. Sarah opened the private residential gate which doubled as access to the mooring dock. Up to thirty to forty boats lay docked on the crystal waters. Inviting, too inviting. Flynn went into Werewolf mode, he looked up at the full moon, growled and discharged a dehumanised howling. Hamish bellowed out a giant laugh, "Fuck me, Flynn! Are you like this every time there's a full moon out?" Flynn was now in state of surrealism, the LSD had taken him to the place of the Werewolf sailor man. "Follow me," as he howled again and took off sprinting down the dock. He began uncovering a few yachts and skiffs until *'Bingo'*, he couldn't believe his luck, a four-man skiff with an outboard engine ready to rock. "Ahoy me Hearties!" as he belted out another giant howling. "All aboard! All aboard!" roared Hamish. Flynn held the rope tight to the mooring as Hamish boarded the two girls. Flynn knew nothing about boats but the outboard motor was akin to starting an old petrol lawnmower, *'sure Jaysus how tough can it be.'*? He yanked it up once and got a small reverberation. He forced it up again and this time got a splutter. Third time and she began humming. *'Fuckin' brilliant.'* Flynn had never driven a car or any mechanically propelled vehicle in his life, bumper cars at the Bray fair excluded. He was now in command of a motor propelled skiff and three passengers while off his head on LSD. Quite the baptism of fire. Once he figured out the rudder blade, they set off full steam ahead under the bridge and towards the River Liffey sluice gates. They all screamed like liberated animals. The wind bellowing through their hair and no life jackets. Flynn managed to manoeuvre the boat around in a semicircle to more screams. *'Faster ye bleedin' gobshite ye!'* Flynn sped up full tilt and angled the boat in line with the shore. All the lights from all the apartments and offices were dancing across the tranquillity of the quay, but to Flynn they felt like alien spaceship invaders which had landed on earth. "The last thing I want to see is any more of them slimy green alien bastards," roared Flynn. He sped up to full speed ahead. The spray was at least comforting from the inferno inside his body. The frantic escape on foot down Nassau street had done nothing to cool his body temperature. Suddenly, Flynn felt the outboard motor lock and straighten. Their weight in the boat was dragging it towards the dock and collision with the bridge.

"Get the fuck off the boat!" roared Flynn, "Get off this fuckin' boat now!" "Code Red, Code bleedin' Red!" he raised the decibel level even further. "We're gonna fuckin' crash." Hamish grabbed Sarah and leapt. Elizabeth looked at Flynn with crazy eyes, "a swim will do us good, c'mon, Daryl."

Flynn

They jumped and landed in the icy water. Flynn was the last off the skiff, like a good Captain. He felt his nostrils and lungs fill up with water straight away. They were only ten metres from shore. He saw the rest of them swimming ahead of him, *'Fuck this, I'm not dying out here tonight.'* He began thrashing around towards the shore. He could hear Hamish laughing as he gasped for air and spat water. Hamish's laughter made Flynn laugh himself and he began to swallow more water. Seconds later, the skiff hit the corner of the Charlotte Quay bridge with a thundering impact. The four seafaring revolutionaries climbed onto the dock and began the most liberated laughter of their lives. The skiff began to take on water. They laughed some more, Hamish making a variety of farmyard animal noises. "So much for steady hand on the fuckin' tiller, Flynn!" They lay on the dock paralysed with laugher. A few minutes away from either being arrested or dying of hypothermia. It was time to get inside. Flynn looked up to see another alien shouting at them from a balcony. This creature was luminous green and seemed to be speaking squeaky alien speak. Unlike the last two aliens in Judge Roy Beans, Flynn found this alien funny and fuelled further fire of his laughter. They made for the ground floor entrance and bid adieu to their beloved skiff which was now about to disappear underneath the icy ripples. "Rest in Peace!" roared Hamish.

Flynn

Chapter Thirteen: Jerusalem & Clockwork Orange

Having exhausted every sinew of orgasmic pleasure, Flynn had decided to call it a day. He adjourned to Hamish's lodgings where he had borrowed a new t-shirt, drank two cans of Bavaria during a laughter-ridden debrief and was now heading out for Round Two. His phone was waterlogged and presumed dead after the Charlotte Quay skiff adventure but Hamish promised to join him in the Pav as back-up in a couple of hours. "Enchant them, Matey," he roared after Flynn with a cacophony of laughter. "Warm them up and I'll see you soon." Flynn bounded through campus to attend a function which he was scarcely invited to.

The Pavilion Bar in Trinity or affectionately known as 'the Pav' rose like Kilimanjaro above the playing fields of Trinity. It was the epicentre of the high achieving sports clubs. Captains and presidents boards hung proudly on wooden structures around the bar bearing the names of high achieving alumni. Those lucky enough to be indoctrinated into Trinity sports folklore paved a well-beaten path for their descendants and those of similar pedigree. It also served as a warning to trespassers or pretenders from outside the golden circles that the core fabric of Trinity belonged to members only. There were certain traditions bespoke to clubs and societies which were the preserve of the select few. 'Knighthoods' and college 'pinks' handed out to only those capable of preserving the bloodline. An underground movement. The Hockey Club was seeped in tradition and it was the juggernaut of their historical significance which made them untouchable. Hockey clubrooms on campus still harboured a journal of all the escapades of previous squadrons on their hockey tours. The details of their collective mayhem and clandestine traditions on foreign shores. That exclusive old boys club. Manna from the Gods for the chosen few, the recipients of their Olympic torch of entitlement. No Rubicon to cross, no foreign lands to conquer. Stay in the mould and honour the 'Legends' of the past. They will be the ones who will attend the graduate jamborees and soak up the adulation of after dinner speeches about their past glories before writing big cheques. Their addiction of seeing the admiring faces of the undergraduates, reinvigorating their status as the founding fathers. Bullshit pseudonyms that only those within their precious circle dare call them by, a rite of passage. All designed to keep Flynn and his ilk at arm's length.

Flynn rounded the border pathway between the rugby and cricket playing fields. He could hear the din of activity in the Pav balcony from a few hundred yards away. The elevation of the Pav structure amplified the noise level. He galloped onwards unperturbed. Once upon a time, he would grimace and wilt in petrification. A stable full of wild horses couldn't drag him into a busy room, let alone a room filled with perceived superiors. Here he was, all alone yet unafraid. The sensation under his feet changed from tarmac to bark mulch as he traversed the runway from the Rugby dressing rooms. The runway of bark mulch led to the sacred rugby turf of College Park where Trinity Rugby played under their nom de guerre 'Dublin University Rugby' and boasted the record as the oldest rugby club in continuous existence in the world. They had their decorated history to preserve and Flynn had his dark history to destroy. Flynn no longer felt any paralysis in his chest, no hyperventilation, no trauma. The death of his inner demons had led to the proliferation of a new army, an army of chaotic neurons running wild inside his mind. He embraced this new phenomenon and welcomed every soldier of fortune who liberated him from his misery. He grew in stature with each and every step. Flynn made landfall on the first rectangular paved step on the outside of the Pav. He looked upwards and saw a few hockey blazers on the main balcony smoking cigarettes and looking smug. They looked downwards towards Flynn as he ascended the historical staircase. Flynn returned their gaze and glared back at them as he grew closer. The first to flinch. They turned away as he hit the second last step before reaching their balcony. The figure of Flynn grew larger and more ominous with every step. "Good evening, gentlemen," said Flynn contemptuously. One of them offered the faintest recognition of a hello by slightly altering the trajectory of his cigarette. This wasn't a welcome but more so a stonewalling, the sort of greeting reserved for trespassers on their hallowed hockey ground. Their little conclave was obviously a splinter group from the main peloton. The three of them almost identical in dress code, hockey blazers over crisp white shirts with double Windsor knotted club ties. Their distinguished vogue was then finished off with beige cord chinos and brown non-slip boat shoes. The three galácticos exuded an air of self-importance. Their facial expressions were quite austere as they surveyed the green lands of the cricket pitch sprawling out ahead of them. Like three nuclear physicists, they hung on each other's every word as if each anecdote held the key to splitting the atom.

In reality, their sober dialogue was limited to what bird had put on a few pounds over the summer as they indiscriminately ogled some of the new Freshers. The crests on their blazers provided the centrifugal force to their popularity. The endorsement of their elitism. It separated them from the rest of the students. A barrier to entry and the preservation of their importance. Their jokes were automatically laughed at before punch lines were even delivered, they were held up as heroes by obsequious hockey wannabes, they were invited to all the big functions and would make speeches at graduate dinners about their forefathers and the legacies that had gone before. These were clones of the past, essential for the continuity of bloodline and pedigree. Flynn strode past them with a wry smile on his face after his greeting was unreciprocated. He now enjoyed this plastic apartheid, he would address later on. Right now, his throat was dry and he needed some libation, the beast in his nature was getting thirsty and calling for alcoholic hydration. The glass frontage of the Pav was only obscured by white wooden frame panels. Flynn gripped the half moon handle at the entrance and pulled the door outwards. The portal to the world of Trinity Hockey lay before him. All these important people and soon to be important people crammed into this bar, all jockeying for position on the social ladder. It would be nights like this where they could make a name for themselves. Flynn made a beeline for the bar and propped his left elbow on the counter in preparation for ordering. The barman took one look at him and said, "it's Hockey Club night tonight, mate" assuming this would be grounds for refusal. He obviously didn't look like your average hockey playing fraternity. Perhaps it was the Clockwork Orange t-shirt he borrowed from Hamish that made him look out of place amongst all these blazers. "Correct! And you're looking at an esteemed club member," Flynn shot back with a smile. "Fair enough," replied the barman with a smile, "what can I get ye? Cans or pints only on the free bar." Flynn briefly surveyed the draft offerings, "I'll have a pint of

Guinness please, Matey." The use of "matey" out of ear shot of Hamish brought a smile to his face. He also thought he should treat himself to a creamy pint of Guinness, since it was free. Flynn overheard the second bar man enquiring in a brief conflab about his eligibility. "He said he was a member so that's good enough for me," he overheard the first barman saying. Obviously he saw the funny side of a rogue imposter gate crashing the exclusive hockey love nest.

The ice-cold creamy pint was put in front of Flynn. He gazed at the contents, temporarily mesmerised by the civil war unfolding within the pint glass. The quashing of a beautiful rebellion as the bubbles were finally brought under control and settled in perfect black formation with a creamy head. He raised the glass aloft as if toasting his invisible dogs of war. His lips were dry and this was the perfect antidote. He lowered the creamy contents down his throat which gave him an almost orgasmic sensation, reminding him of his earlier intercourse with Elizabeth. He placed the pint back on the counter and surveyed less than a quarter left in the glass. He held up the entrails to the barman, "Same again please, Matey." The barman duly obliged and nonchalantly flipped down the Guinness tap, initiating another pour of black gold.

Flynn licked his lips and necked back the remainder of this pint, he then reshaped his body position to survey the room. A Serengeti of megalomaniacs and sycophants lay before him. The 'brown-nosing' Olympics was in full swing. Flynn began to theorise whether this was indeed a race to the top or a race to the bottom as another creamy pint appeared on the counter beside him. He could feel the funny looks being shot across the room like scud missiles, "like who the fuck is that guy with the Clockwork Orange t-shirt?" Flynn took another prolonged gulp of Guinness and decided to get his nicotine fix. This time he had his very own lighter and a new box of Marlboro Lights, Hamish had been good enough to stock him up from his extensive stash of cigarettes he procured from his last trip to Spain. Flynn exhaled a long plume of smoke across the revellers. He could feel two very specific sets of eyes trained on him. The eyes of Nick Brewster and Charlie Stokes, the vanquished pair from Judge Roy Beans.

All the blazers present had already attended a swanky dinner in the dining hall before congregating in the Pav. They had already got their 'slim jim' glass of Guinness and a three-course meal in preparation for mixing with the rest of the hockey proletariat. A couple of hours glorifying themselves and toasting their own importance with copious bottles of fine red wine was the perfect preparation for more adulation. They had worked up an appetite by observing pre-dinner grace in Latin and belting out a stirring rendition of 'Jerusalem' before gleefully sitting down to feast.

All the blazers walked up together in a marching convoy that wouldn't have looked out of place on the 12th of July. Brewster and Stokes had been perturbed over the altercation in Judge Roy Beans from the night before but had resigned themselves that the perpetrators were obviously a couple of riff-raff and moved on. Now, seeing one of the aggressors sinking free pints of Guinness in the inner circle of their hockey enclave was a traumatic sight to say the least. Flynn leaned back on the bar with a look of contentment on his face, he racked up another Guinness and a cigarette hung from his lips. He exhaled deeply as he pondered the inner death of Daryl Flynn. For the first time in his life he felt completely liberated, yesterday's rampage had unveiled a dormant beast inside his soul. Now the beast had come out to play. The past twenty-four hours had seen an evolution inside of Daryl Flynn, suicide without the rigmarole of a funeral. He was still alive and the Guinness and cigarettes were spectacular. He had made love to a beautiful woman earlier and pleasured her in ways he didn't even know existed. Now he leant back on the bar, donning a Clockwork Orange t-shirt, fearlessly surveying a room full of far superior human beings. He allowed himself another smile as he gestured to the barman to stick on another pint.

Flynn

Chapter Fourteen: "Up to Our Knees in Fenian Blood"

Flynn caught sight of a blazer approaching him from his left side. It was Andrew Magnier. "Ah Jaysus it's himself!" said Flynn extending his hand and offering a broad smile, "I'll tell ye one thing brother I'm getting great value for that bleedin' fiver," Flynn continued with a grand exhalation of smoke as he choked down a gigantic slug of Guinness. Magnier was done up like a kipper, perfect blazer and tie etiquette. On the face of it a clone of the others but there was that something about him. He didn't move like the others or seem to crave attention. He seemed like an ordinary dude. He accepted Flynn's handshake and smiled back, "Ah great stuff man, glad you came along, by the way, I'm Andrew, eh… Andrew Magnier…" He hesitated at the final furlong of introduction knowing that his formalised hockey greeting was frivolous at best. "Flynn!" barked Flynn with an assertive smile, he crunched down on their handshake whilst maintaining eye contact and perfectly balancing his cigarette between his left canine and lower lip. Magnier had remembered making Flynn's acquaintance the day before, the rest of hockey stand had chastised him about inviting Flynn to the Hockey drinks. Flynn had stood before them, hunched over, incapable of making eye contact and staring at the ground. His claret red face had given away the fact that he didn't belong there, not in Trinity College and certainly not in the Hockey club.

"Hey Magnier, are you in charge of the freak academy? Didn't the Goonies have a guy like him living in their basement, anyone else you want to invite?" goaded Marlowe as he entertained the masses on the Hockey stand. Flynn had been an easy target and was still within ear shot, not that Marlowe cared about whose feelings he hurt. Ross Marlowe only cared about himself, his profile and his own importance. Flynn had overheard himself being ridiculed, he knew it was that Marlowe prick, but couldn't decipher the exact wording. The cacophony of laughter said it all, Flynn was an easy target, another humiliation.

Magnier had refused to join in the banter. By the looks of things, Flynn had a tough life and he wasn't about to make it any worse. Magnier found it hard to calibrate Flynn, he assumed this was a mission of mercy, a few minutes small talk with a proper outsider. He felt bad about the previous day, he had a soft nature and deep down supported the underdog. Schadenfreude wasn't his thing. "Eh… How's Trinity treating you, Flynn?" he enquired. Flynn took another elongated sup of his pint. "So far so good, got high as a kite last night, robbed a boat and had sex all day long." He then inhaled even more deeply and purposely as he summoned up another giant plume of smoke which exited through his smiling teeth. Flynn glared into the pupils of Magnier's eyes. He wanted to hate him but something was holding him back. Magnier held his gaze and Flynn could see a certain empathy within. He looked like the rest of them but he was nothing like the rest of them. "Sounds like you're on top form," said Magnier with a jovial laugh, but he was on edge. He felt the emission of Flynn's psychic energy, like a volcano about to erupt, it was a matter of time. "How is Trinity treating you, Andrew Magnier? Can I call you Andrew, Andy, Magnier or have you a preference?" Flynn was suddenly overcome by the feeling of humiliation from the previous day, an anger ignited inside him. "Having a grand time so far, man… and call me Andy," said Magnier. "And by the way, I'm sorry if you felt awkward yesterday, there's a few of this lot with a very high opinion of themselves." offered Magnier contritely. He was backpedalling but the ominous glare of Flynn had forced him into addressing the issue. Flynn erupted in laughter, his chest cavity vibrating wildly as he took another long, ponderous pull of his cigarette and repeated what he'd just heard."... A high opinion of themselves... A high fuckin' opinion of themselves! And did your mates have a good laugh at me yesterday, Andy? Is that what ye do, go around laughing at fuckers below you on the social food chain?" Flynn was beginning to get his gander up. His anger was bubbling beneath the surface, however, as he retained his relaxed posture on the bar counter, both his elbows still anchoring his stance.

Magnier realised that his next sentence would be the difference between a box in the snot and a stay of execution. The stay of execution being continuity in this mesmerising conversation. Magnier had only one option, he had to go on the offensive. "Listen here man, I don't laugh at anyone, I don't give a fuck about social food chains or fellas living off pretention, that's not me, I take people at face value." Flynn held his stare. A brief silence descended, the perfect face off. Flynn looked probingly through Magnier for any sign of bullshit and to Magnier's credit he maintained eye contact. The perfect irony. A hockey blazer explaining himself to a 'yellowpacker' in a Clockwork Orange t-shirt. "You're a sound fucker, Andy," said Flynn, he shunted himself to his full height and put an arm around him. "Let me get you a creamy pint of stout." Flynn turned to the barman and called for "two creamy pints of Guinness please, barman." Heineken was Magnier's tipple, but now wasn't the time to get precious.

Flynn

Brewster and Stokes looked at each other in bewilderment as they surveyed one of their own locked in convivial conversation with the maniac from the night before. Not just one of their own but one of the Magnier family, one of the most formidable families in the country and a cornerstone of Trinity Hockey tradition. "Get one of them down the hatch too," Flynn ushered a cigarette into Magnier's mouth, a casual smoker at best but he accepted nonetheless. Flynn extended him the inferno lighter which drew a chuckle from Magnier. "There goes the eyebrows anyway," as he wheezed a gentle drag through his laughter. Magnier knew he didn't have to hang around with this maniac but there was a certain magnetic intrigue about Flynn. The snap evolution of character change in twenty-four hours fascinated him. Magnier clinked glasses with Flynn and took a long swill of Guinness.

"Your good health, Sir." Flynn remoulded himself to the perfect relaxed position on the bar counter. He could sense a certain nervous energy inside Magnier. He enjoyed this sensation of power, that he could suddenly manipulate the emotions of others. He had spent his life hugging shadows in the darkness and avoiding conflict. Now he was like a behemoth, bereft of fear and boundaries. Flynn thought about his life, his old life and the people who knew him or thought they knew him. Daryl Fuckin' Flynn! The thoughts of the old Daryl Flynn gave him a sickening feeling inside his stomach. It gave him so much satisfaction knowing that he killed that pathetic mess of a human being. That character who humiliated him since his earliest memory. He necked back nearly three quarters of his remaining pint as if to cleanse himself of the very thoughts of his old self.

"No messing with you, some man to sink a pint!" said Magnier. "Just keeping the demons at bay," retorted Flynn and flashed him a devilish grin. Flynn arched himself nonchalantly back towards the bar. "Two more Guinness please, Matey, and can you give us two Sambucas as well please?" The barman was mildly entertained by the bizarre cameo but briefly made eye contact with Magnier to make sure he wasn't being held against his will. His gaze going to Magnier then back to Flynn and briefly to Magnier again before procuring the drinks. "Early doors for that man, I'll be howling at the moon at this rate," Magnier flushed back the remainder of his pint to make room for the latest onslaught. He already had a good drink inside him, and was rapidly approaching the precipice. The sambucas appeared first. The whiff of liquorice petroleum filling their nostrils. Flynn set both shot glasses ablaze. The perfect blue flame bounced around in its own perfect autonomy. "Rise and shine, Andy… rise and shine!" he handed Magnier his Sambuca engulfed in mini inferno. They gently clinked glasses, blew out the Sambuca and downed the shots. Flynn gave his glass an educated lick before consumption but Magnier overlooked this small technicality and scalded his lips. He recoiled in pain as he felt immediate swelling and blistering on his lower lip, coupled with the chemical reaction inside his bowls. His eyes watered involuntarily as the swanky three-course meal from early evening showed the first signs of rebellion inside his gut. His mouth cupped into a giant 'O' shape as he threw the glass back on the counter. The pints of Guinness arrived and Magnier downed his like a man possessed, eager to alleviate the mini forest fire on his lip. The touch of the ice-cold glass on his lips was redemption in itself. However, the lack of synchronisation of his swollen lips precipitated a black trickle of Guinness to dive straight down his crisp white shirt. "Same again, please, Matey!" said Flynn with renewed zest. Magnier felt the moisture on his white shirt and quickly deciphered that he had a Guinness stained shirt to go with his Mick Jagger lips. "And don't forget to lick the glass this time, Andy!" as they burst out laughing together. The next shots arrived and both dispatched them down the hatch with renewed vigour. They toasted their pints of Guinness. Magnier looked at him with increasing bamboozlement. "Louis, I think this is the beginning of a beautiful friendship."

Magnier's father Gerard and Grandad William both attended Trinity College and played Hockey with distinction. The giant mahogany Captain's board featured both their names. The hockey and rugby boards were the most grandiose and prominent features of the Pav. Ascension to commander in chief of either club guaranteed immortality. A place in history where the "made-men" of the past could look down upon the current incumbents forever more. Like the mafia, there was a code of omertà with the innermost workings of the Hockey club. There was a bloodline to be preserved. They were formidable businessmen and had the ability to command every room they walked into. Andrew Magnier had attended copious family functions where the theme was dominated by his father and grandfather toasting each other's legendary achievements. Their stories of their Herculean victories grew legs over time, the detail and delivery became even more inflated as each year rolled on. Christmastime became an exercise in the self-indulgence of their egos. His Dad and Grandad would position themselves by the fireplace after dinner and down glasses of 18-year-old Macallan Sherry. They had a quota of stories to get through and it was considered blasphemy not to hang on their every word. Their nostalgia would extend to how their business deals were struck, how they conquered the market and acquired major portfolios. However, the stories would always come back to their success on the hockey pitch and the admiration of their peers. Their tales would often jump to the third person to accentuate their importance and impact on their generation. The level of ingratiation used to make Magnier nauseous. Bearing the Magnier name was a rite of passage but also a burden. With it came an expectation and underlying pressure to live up to his forefathers. There was no room to breathe, the name was suffocating. His family crest decorated the wall of his school and now the family name decorated the wall of his University. Even in the college bar the name looked down on him as he had a few pints. He had been presented with a hockey blazer the first day he set foot on the cobble lock of front square. He was immediately promoted to the first team squad without a trial and invited to every club function because he was "royalty." He was big and robust, a decent 'link' midfielder, but not elite standard. He was the eldest of the grandchildren to attend Trinity College, the next great bearer of the Magnier Olympic torch. The Magniers were power brokers of Trinity Hockey. They sponsored the team, bankrolled the club and always made speeches at club functions. Magnier appreciated the fact that he was from money but never saw himself as the product of money.

Magnier's drunken gaze wandered to the Captain's board. He was genuinely enjoying Flynn's company and vice versa. "Do you see that board up there, Flynn," said Magnier as he gesticulated towards the giant mahogany Hockey board bearing the names of the Hockey Club Captains. Flynn turned his head and surveyed the wooden structure whilst exhaling another plume of smoke and offering Magnier another cigarette, which he accepted gratefully.

"That board up there has my Dad and my Grandad's name written in stone," he paused as a wave of emotion infiltrated his voice, he took a drag of his cigarette and exhaled as if temporarily trying to compose himself. "And they want me to be a Magnier just like them… just like fuckin' them…" his voice tailed off as he orated the last few words. "Do you know what it's like coming to a place like this being a fuckin' Magnier… everyone wants to be your friend because your Dad bankrolls the fuckin' place." Magnier paused for a momentary introspection. Flynn was in no mood for a heart-to-heart with the entitled glitterati. "Try being Daryl Fuckin' Flynn!" he quipped, "Give us a shout if ye fancy a swap, I've a Iovely single bed in a council house with your name on it. Now here! Get that down the hatch," he thrust another flaming Sambuca into Magnier's hand, "and lick the fuckin' glass this time!"

Flynn was still on his own mission. A quick clink and another Hiroshima slid down the hatches of both men. Magnier grimaced and recovered a smile, the contents of his three-course dinner nestling in his gut began to stir violently. Flynn looked him up an down, "Are you okay there, Kemo Sabe? You're like a fella about to blow a head gasket?" Magnier grimaced. The rebellion had now become a fully fledged army and it was a matter of time before they would make a Dunkirk style landing in the nearest toilet bowl. "I'm grand now, yeah," Magnier furiously swallowed saliva in a vain attempt to keep the cobblestones at bay. He tried to turn his attention back to the Captain's board and continued, "They want me to be just like them," but Magnier was on the clock, the Royal Navy in his gut had signalled their intention for warfare, he had minutes, maybe seconds to get into the Pav toilets before detonation. "Fuck! Here, Flynn, will you hold my jacket? Need to run a quick errand." Magnier handed his coat to Flynn, undid his double Windsor knot tie and disappeared into the sanctuary of the Pav toilet.

Flynn held Magnier's blazer and allowed himself a wry smile. The perfect fabric, freshly pressed and dry-cleaned, the tapestry of the breast pocket pristinely sewed together. He could smell Magnier's expensive aftershave and it sure as hell wasn't Lynx Africa. Only the inner circle were allowed to wear such a distinguished garment. He wasn't just holding a jacket, he was holding the personification of acceptance. *'Fuck it! In for a penny, in for a pound,'* Flynn reminded himself. Sure wasn't Magnier of similar build. Flynn rested his pint back down on the counter and pursed his lips in preparation for an extended retention of his cigarette. Flynn slipped his right arm into the jacket and felt the silk inner lining envelop his forearm and snake its way to his shoulder. He inverted his left arm behind his back and searched blindly for the same silk feel. The blazer briefly became taut as his left arm navigated the final journey to his shoulder. The lapels were pointed skywards as if in protest at the commandeering of this sacred fabric by an outsider. Flynn flattened them down without any grand ceremony, fixed the collar and for the coup-de-grace smoothed both hands down the double-breasted centre and buttoned it closed. He exhaled longingly through a broad smile and stood upright. This perfectly tailored blazer, underpinned by a Clockwork Orange t-shirt. Perhaps standards in the hockey club were dropping. And not just anyone's blazer, this garment belonged to royalty. A hushed silence descended on the Pav as the sustained tapping of a spoon against a wine glass cut through the noise. The gathering all turned to face the noise. Many in the gathering knew full well what was coming next. It was time for a few colloquial hockey anthems to ramp up the emotions and pay homage to the sacred crest. The great unwashed amongst them stood in childlike expectation as the spectacle unfolded. Nobody embodied the great unwashed more so than Flynn, decked out in a buttoned blazer and intrigued by the impending recital. Stokes mounted a long bar stool with great dexterity, his head nearly touching the ceiling. He held in his arms aloft which raised a cheer which nearly lifted the roof off. He reminded Flynn of one of his great childhood heroes, 'Macho Man Randy Savage' of WWF acclaim would mount the top rope of the ring and seemingly jump into outer space before landing on his opponent and rendering him concussed. Stokes, however, had no such delusions of violence. His objective was simply to belt out a few anthems. His lowered his arms to initiate quiet which was immediately granted. He put his finger on his lips to reinforce the necessity for pure silence as not a sound was heard, apart from the dry retching reverberations of Magnier who was still confined to Pav toilet duty trying to extricate his intestines from the swanky three-course meal of early evening. Once Stokes commanded the full room to his satisfaction, he became quickly animated. Showtime! He lowered his hands in a contrived trembling motion and beckoned everyone to follow suit;

"Ooooooooooooooooooooooooooooooooooooh…" the build up was interminable but served to ramp up the atmosphere even more.

"If I had the wings of a sparrow, if I had the arse of a crow,
I'd fly over UCD college and shit on the fuckers below… Below!
Shit on… Oh, shit on… Oh, Shit on the fuckers below… Below!"
Shit on… Oh, shit on… Oh, Shit on the fuckers below… Below!"

After a hiatus of a few seconds, it was time for his second helping. This time with the added stimulus of being handed a pint and knocking back most of the contents. In fairness to Stokes, he was a showman and knew how to whip them into a frenzy.

"I parked my tractor in Belfield Park doodah, doodah,
I parked my tractor in Belfield Park doodah, doodah day"
Couldn't get the points! Couldn't get the points! I parked
My tractor in Belfield park doodah, doodah day!"

This was followed by a cacophony of cheering which erupted into orbit as Brewster mounted another stool beside him for the impending duet. The Pav became a zoo of emotion. The sense of belonging and ridiculing of the UCD goons added another layer of superiority to the faithful gathered before them. And then it really kicked off as both in unison gave another perfect intro with trembling hands:

"Oooooooooooooooooooooooooooooooooooooh…"
"Hello! Hello! We are the Trinners boys!"
Hello! Hello! You'll hear us by our noise,
Up to our knees in Fenian blood,
Surrender or you'll die,
Cause we are the Trinners marching boys!"

Now, this really blew the roof off the Pav. Three encores of the same verse later and there was hardly a blood vessel left in anyone's neck. Tears were nearly shed as the glitterati amongst the blazers linked arms in trojan solidarity. Flynn leaned back on the bar and marvelled at the spectacle. He had disembowelled another pint of Guinness during the festivities and already had another fresh one setting on the counter. 'Some value for a fiver,' he reiterated to himself. He inhaled deeply and smiled as he patted his pristinely pressed blazer. Brewster and Stokes were mobbed by the expectant crowd as they made their way from the stools back down to planet earth. They soaked up the adulation with every stride. Both got a giant embrace from the boy wonder Marlowe, his endorsement of their legendary status adding further endorsement to their invincibility. They fervently embraced each other before talk turned to some irritating business at hand.

Flynn's presence had not gone unnoticed. His fiendish decimation of pints of Guinness and Sambucas without breaking stride had similarly been noted. His tenuous association with Magnier had been written off as a mission of mercy. Magnier's charity was obviously misplaced cavorting with this vermin. Brewster and Stokes had hawked him since he set foot in the joint.

Magnier finally emerged from his sabbatical. His swanky three-course meal now permanently disembodied and residing in the Pav's underground system. He laughed as he caught sight of Flynn masquerading around in his unique style of club blazer and Clockwork Orange t-shirt. "Jaysus it's about time you showed up, I was worried about getting stopped by the fashion police on the way home." Flynn handed the blazer back to Magnier, "Thanks man, you wear it well!" he said, "now I better make tracks back to our table before they send out a search party, I'll chat to you in a while Flynn," after a brief cordial hand-slap Magnier returned to the dark abyss of the social strata, his double Windsor knot and blazer perfectly affixed once more. He had displayed enough off the cuff emotion for one night. Flynn was on his own once again.

Flynn

Chapter Fifteen: The Ginger Man

It wasn't long before a new blazer emerged on the horizon, this one not quite so cordial and the bearer of a more ominous message. Marlowe had an entourage everywhere he went, a certain magnetism which comes with a prodigy from opulence. He was always surrounded by either 'hangers-on' from St. Andrew's College school, Trinity hockey fraternisers or a mixture of both. But never on his own. Marlowe never knew the feeling of trying to enjoy his own company over a coffee or eating his lunch on his own. He never knew the life of solitude and how some people would put on a brave face whilst eating their sandwich alone, trying desperately to distract themselves reading a newspaper or book. He would eliminate someone from his entourage depending on his mood. Like the pied piper, he could call whatever tune he wanted and the loyal rats would follow. There was an aura around him and everyone fed into it. Marlowe splintered away slightly from his entourage and approached Flynn, his confrères gathered around to hear his verbal onslaught. "Well, if it's not the star of the Goonies," said Marlowe, "I see someone has finally found the key to the basement and let you loose! Now tell me, sloth-man, what the fuck are you doing here?" A cacophony of laughter erupted from the tag-alongs as they embraced each other to accentuate the humour of his words. Flynn had been in quite a happy place before this frivolous contretemps, however, suddenly the vulnerable feelings of St. Davids came flooding back. The bullying, the fear and the hiding in the shadows. He leaned back on the bar counter, smiled and visualised his next actions. "You've no business here you fuckin' degenerate, you're not one of us and never will be, now drink up and fuck off." Flynn caught sight of a now familiar silhouette through the glass doors. Always one to make an entrance. "What? Are you some kind of fuckin' autistic mute, finish your drink and fuck off!" Marlowe recognised this was all one way traffic, he had entertained the masses enough and given them enough sound bites to be rehashed over hilarious coffee tomorrow morning. The only one who wasn't impressed was with this conduct was Sophie, his prospective number two for the night. "Ah, cheer the fuck up," he bellowed, as he slapped her on the shoulder, a lot harder than would warrant affection. She recoiled. The Marlowe fan club doubled down in a circle to glorify what they'd just heard. "Ah fuck it I'm off to the John," said Marlowe as he sauntered nonchalantly across the wooden floor towards the Pav toilets. Flynn followed his every step as Hamish appeared at the doorway, no doubt well imbibed from his earlier evening's antics in the dorm. "Aye, Aye, Sweetheart," as he grabbed Flynn in a bear hug and planted a big kiss on his cheek, "I've been up to mischief, chalk me down one of them Guinness and I'll tell you all about it," said Hamish in typical gregarious fashion. "Not just yet brother, you'll have to fuckin' earn it," said Flynn with a devilish laugh, "follow me!"

Hamish knew Flynn meant business. A wide grin lit up his face. He could see the ominous and unhinged look in Flynn's eyes. He had seen it before. That unmistakable pupil dilation, the mutation from Flynn to Werewolf. Hamish flashed a cursory glance out the Pav window to check if this metamorphosis was the result of a full moon or simply the flotilla of alcohol Flynn had just consumed. Flynn's relaxed poise changed, he stubbed out his cigarette and stood to his full height like the Rougarou emerging from a swamp. Flynn strode calmly towards the Pav toilets, a sadistic grin decorated his face. He stopped and briefly turned to Hamish, "Oh and just in case you're wondering… this pox bottle fuckin' deserves what's coming to him." Hamish sniggered in anticipation "I don't doubt it, Matey, who am I to question your integrity," his sniggering turned to a more bellowing laugh and he sparked up a cigarette. Marlowe was about to learn a life lesson. Flynn made the sharp left turn from the bar down the dimly lit narrow hall to the toilets. He had a brief moment of introspection. He no longer felt like Daryl Flynn, all emotional connection with his past life was severed within his soul. His nerves, social anxiety and lack of self-worth, all the humiliating things which had dominated his pathetic existence, were missing. He still had the memories, but no longer the feelings. The irrepressible force within was driving him towards a new destiny. Perhaps he was out of control, but what control did he have before? There was absolutely nothing in Daryl Flynn's life that he had to lose. Marlowe stood at the urinal, a subtle sway of his hips accentuating the nonchalance that he approached everything in life. He was alone. No entourage. He whistled casually to himself as he thought about what bird he would be bringing back to hockey rooms later. He had the pick of the bunch. He inwardly flicked through the few candidates in his mind and resolved himself that Sophie would be the best bet, as she would definitely "put out" on the first night. This brief reminder of the power he wielded brought a smile to his face. He'd go back out to his posse, soak in more adulation, up the ante on the flirtation with Sophie and quietly bring her back to his pad on campus. He reminded himself to be vigilant around who saw them leaving together. He couldn't be seen to be a "taken man". He intended to sleep with at least two other easy targets before the week was out.

Flynn

Marlowe gently caressed the foreskin of his penis as he relieved himself of the last few drops of urine. He double-checked for any splashes on his non-slip boat shoes before reaching down and slowly buttoning up his beige chinos. He then folded across his double-breasted blazer and affixed the gold crested buttons to complete the perfect look. As usual, he paid little attention to his surrounds as he swivelled the couple of yards to the handwash basin and gave his hands an expeditious rinse. It was only when he looked conceitedly at himself in the mirror that he spotted Flynn over his shoulder. Flynn leaned against the cubicle with folded arms. He appeared relaxed yet every blood cell had taken up position on his outer epidermis in preparation for this brief assault. "Ah, Mr. Goonies how's it hanging?" said Marlowe with typical condescension. Marlowe's routine scorn for anyone below him on the food chain fed into his sense of invincibility. Anybody outside the blazer fraternity or similar social standing were vermin in his eyes. He even viewed most of his entourage with contempt, simply a band of masseurs for his substantial ego, despite coming from economically advantaged schools like himself. His sanctimonious path was laid out before him. He had no conscience. His life had been a runaway train of success, an unchecked upward curve. He looked at Flynn as the lowest common denominator, a sub culture, a rat. The sort of degenerate that would maintain the family gardens and cut the grass. He knew Flynn was the wrong social strata and therefore the lowest rung of the ladder. Marlowe observed Flynn for a brief moment. "So is this what you do, clean the toilets for a living?" he sneered and cleared his throat with a laugh. Flynn maintained his glare, an unblemished grin still lit up his face. He gently pivoted off the cubicle door and slowly advanced towards the handwash basin. "I have to hand it to you, Marlowe, you're consistent to the very end. Think of this moment as a purification. A time for reflection." The beast inside of Flynn was spiralling, it was a matter of seconds. His muscles contracted into perfect fight poise. His eyes narrowed and he tightened both fists. "Kill or be killed, Marlowe," Flynn's mouth formed a feral snarl. He was now within striking distance. Marlowe turned to face him. He was on the verge of barking out an expletive ridden rant when the first assault landed, a thunderclap perfectly executed with both fists simultaneously to the side of the head. Marlowe recoiled from the powerful impact, bamboozled as a flatline tone escalated through his head. Dazed, he knew Flynn was talking but the high-pitched electric humming drowned out his words. He also heard a third-party laughing near the toilet door but it was echoed and distant. One or perhaps both eardrums now perforated. Flynn repeated the same striking action to both sides of his head, this time even more concussive. The black cirrus clouds began to form around Marlowe's vision. "And that concludes your long-overdue lobotomy, Marlowe, now it's time for your baptism to cleanse you of all sin." His strategy was not to disfigure Marlowe but merely traumatize him, to bring him to the darkest part of the forest and look the beast in the eyes. "Fingers crossed the plumbing in this kip is up to scratch, oh, and I'd like you to meet my lovely assistant - Dr. Hamish." Flynn and Hamish grabbed Marlowe under the groin, raised him aloft and backed him into the cubicle.

Marlowe screamed as the angle of his non-slip boat shoes went above horizontal and then perpendicular to the toilet ceiling. His semi-conscious state suddenly awakening as his demise grew nearer. He was suspended in midair, locked in a perfect spear tackle, he tried in vain to extricate his head from the inside of the ceramic toilet bowl. Flynn held down the flush lever and laughed as Marlowe's head became submerged in the scoured pit of grotesqueness. The Pav toilets never drained on the first attempt. On foot of the traffic congestion and overworked nature of the student bar toilets, they would simply block till on the verge of flooding before gently emptying on a slow trickle. Hamish erupted in a volcano of laughter. The cigarette perched on his lips, he held Marlowe's other leg on the left side of Flynn. Marlowe's hockey blazer was draped over his head as his tie dangled over his nasal passage down his forehead. Once Flynn engaged the flush, the full cistern emptied into the blocked up toilet boil. Marlowe's terror screams became more pronounced but were drowned out by the music and cacophony of noise inside the bar. He suddenly became dehumanized as the water level rose over his head and he involuntarily inhaled the despicable toilet backwash. He fought in vain trying to grip the outer bowl but gravity granted him no leverage. He was drowning. "He's fuckin' drowning, Matey!" said Hamish calmly, more matter-of-factly than out of concern for the ignominious demise of Marlowe. Flynn and Hamish fished him up for air as he hyperventilated and coughed. They laid him on the cubicle floor on his side as he gasped and accelerated into a full on panic attack. Flynn stood over him laughing, "Do ye want a loan of a t-shirt, Matey?" Marlowe was glued to the floor. His hyperventilation interrupted only by a violent vomiting, upon which he further smeared himself in. His crisp white shirt, blazer and hockey tie were decimated, the symbols of power hanging limply on the toilet floor. Flynn knelt down closely beside Marlowe and whispered in his ear. "It's OK brother… They still love you out there and let's face it you can afford the dry cleaning bill, think of this as Jesus giving you another chance," as he erupted into laughter. A traumatised Marlowe was frozen in shock on the cubicle floor. Meanwhile, a member of Marlowe's fan club waited outside for his re-emergence, she was a fresher trying to make a big impression. Short skirt, tanned and all the right features. The perceived road to popularity being to infiltrate the inner circle of power. Her favoured member of that inner circle of power now lying prostrate on the cubicle floor covered in baptismal Pav backwash. Hamish eyed the innocent hockey wannabe upon exit. "Aye, Aye, Tiger! I don't think he will be out in any hurry but you're welcome to join us if ye want?" He ushered her towards the bar where Flynn had already gestured for two fresh pints of Guinness.

Flynn

Chapter Sixteen: The Gingerman's Last Stand

Sophie Longhurst was from Cheltenham. A very bright, good-looking girl with a blind spot for hooking up with narcissists. Her taste in boyfriends always seemed to bely her intelligence and normal intuition. She was vulnerable to the charm of successful sports-people. For some reason, her insecurities became magnified around those who fancied themselves. Ross Marlowe was a prime example. A hockey prodigy and the youngest player to ever win a senior cap for the Irish National Team. His fame extended mainly to the confines of the national hockey fraternity but this was enough to elevate his stature to messianic status in the grounds of Trinity College. It was this status within the micro universe of Trinity which Sophie latched on to. She had a happy childhood and adolescence, she never wanted for anything but mysteriously garnered a certain feeling of inadequacy. Her parents gave her all the love in the world but she never felt herself complete without a boyfriend on her arm, invariably her choice in men was destructive. Her relationships became all-consuming, with an obsession for constant contact and a paranoia around the movements of her boyfriends. Any friends who couldn't stand to listen to her constant ramblings were dropped. Over time, she lost friends, good friends who cared about her. She became an enigma. How could a beautiful-looking girl from money who achieved great grades feel so inadequate.

"Pint of Guinness, Sweetheart?" asked Flynn with a giant grin on his face. "Don't think I'm much 'a Guinness drinker," replied Sophie, a certain psychic energy washing over her, she realised her two new acquaintances were not your atypical hockey patrons. Her intuition sounded the alarm bells, this was red alert and time for evacuation. These were not the sort of characters to be associating with if she wanted to climb the social ladder, yet she felt compelled and intrigued by their company. There was an inexplicable magnetism around their presence. Her gut told her to go back to her table, but she suddenly embodied the moth being sucked into the giant flame. "One Guinness but then I have to go back to my friends," she feigned disinterest, "but make it a glass, thanks." Flynn looked at her with disdain. "We don't do glasses around here! Make that three pints of Guinness please, Barman," he broke his look of contempt, flashed her a smile and lit another cigarette. He offered Sophie a cigarette which she accepted. He flicked the spark wheel of his lighter which was still set on giant flame, she accepted the light by cupping her hands around his. She smiled. Her shoulderless dress hugged her perfectly chiselled, tanned body. Her symmetry embodied a terrestrial paradise. Her sculptured shoulders glistened with the precision of Mount Rushmore. Her flawless legs were endless, the perfect balance of muscle and flesh. It was a white, floral two-piece dress which showcased two inches of perfectly toned muscle on her abdomen above the skirt line. There were no tights to tarnish this beauty, the odd freckle validating her reality, the reincarnation of Helen of Troy. Her brown hair teased her shoulders. She was a moon Goddess of beauty, yet her underlying insecurity made her vulnerable.

"Three pints of Guinness," intercepted the barman as he clunked the pints in a row on the counter. He was completely oblivious to the attempted murder which had just taken place in the neighbouring toilets. The tumultuous din had drowned out the near-death screams of Marlowe. Hamish winked at Flynn and handed Sophie a creamy pint of Guinness.

"Now, my love, think of this as a new beginning." Sophie took the pint in her left hand, her bangle bracelet slipping slightly down her forearm. Everything about her was sexy. "Welcome to the land of the unshackled, the portal of paradise, a wonderland!" Hamish was in full theatrical 'Hamish-mode'. Flynn had that dry throat feeling again. The mixture of retribution, nicotine and toilet bleach had parched the back of this throat. He necked back half his pint and looked ponderously back into the glass whilst wearing a creamy Guinness moustache. Still the feeling of desiccation lingered. He impatiently necked the second half of this pint and called for "three more Guinness" prompting a bewildered look from the bar man who complied nonetheless.

Sophie took a long lingering draft of her pint and allowed herself a smile. It was the first time in the night she didn't feel self-conscious or judged. "So what did you do to him?" she asked with inquisition as opposed to the welfare of Marlowe - her love-quest of only ten minutes ago had evaporated. "The plumbing in this place leaves a lot to be desired," Flynn exhaled as the memory of a few moments ago began to ferment in his mind. "Consider it a purification, a second baptism and a lesson in humility."

Flynn spoke like some deranged zealot after enacting Sharia law. "Oh wait, check me out, when in bleedin' Rome!" Flynn stood forward, commanding further attention. Formulating a phantom gun cocked in his right hand, he deepened his voice, narrowed his eyes and recited the lines, memorised hundreds of times, from his favourite movie; "The path of the righteous man is beset on all sides by the inequities of the selfish and the tyranny of evil men. Blessed is he who, in the name of charity and good will, shepherds the weak through the valley of darkness, for he is truly his brother's keeper and the finder of lost children. And I will strike down upon thee with great vengeance and furious anger those who would attempt to poison and destroy My brothers. And you will know My name is the Lord when I lay My vengeance upon thee."

Flynn fired the full magazine of his phantom gun, complete with sound effects and mock recoil. Hamish ignited in synchronised laughter, "You're the craziest motherfucker on this planet, Flynn," Hamish grabbed him in a hug, cigarette burning brightly in his mouth and looked him in the eyes, "I fuckin' love you man!" prompting more crazed laughter. Sophie couldn't help but laugh at this psychotic spectacle. Her whole world revolved around people who only cared about what the world thought of them. Here were two maniacs who seemed intent on only exploring the darker side of the moon. The next three pints arrived with an identical clunk, Flynn lined them up with geometrical precision and beckoned Sophie to neck back the remnants of her surviving few gulps. She duly complied, her perfectly formed neck tilted backwards and viscerally consumed the remaining contents. Turning back towards her two salivating companions, she ventured: "That is officially the quickest pint I've ever downed." Flynn gave her a wink, "ye can't beat class, Sophie, ye can't beat class," prompting more laughter.

They divvied out the next round of pints, Hamish looked at Flynn and said, "you know what time it is," in perfect synchronisation they raised their glasses and roared in defiance - "Viva la Revolución!" Sophie joined them in the toast. "You know, I'm delighted I met you guys," she said with a broad smile. "Enchanté," said Hamish, executing another cameo of elegance as he kissed her on the hand. Flynn beamed a smile but he stood transfixed on the door. This was not over yet.

In the next room there was a different type of renaissance in progress. Marlowe still squirmed in an involuntary fetal position, he had soiled his beige slacks so was now in perfect symmetry from top to bottom. The violent stench still suffocated his lungs, every last morsel from his bowls had been evacuated and now he sporadically convulsed, like an epileptic in the final throes of a seizure. His body had prepared for death and the after effects were devastating. Those two maniacs had submerged him in the flooded toilet bowl. "Drown him in the fuckin' Khazi!" replayed through his head. The sinister laughter. Those fuckin' maniacs. The feeling of vulnerability as he tried in vain to extricate himself from the jaws of death. Marlowe raised his head a few inches off the floor but an adhesive mucous slime still bound his forehead to the toilet surface. The slime was a cosmopolitan mix of everything a student toilet had to offer. He wiped it away with his right hand which only transferred the gloop to his fingers. The abhorrent sight forced him to dry retch again. The ringing in his ears had slightly subsided, he raised his left hand to his ear and wiped away the excess fluid, he brought his hand back in front of his face for inspection and saw claret red blood on his hand. His ear drum had burst which precipitated the bamboozlement. Through the electric humming he could still hear the din of revellers outside in the bar ramping up the intensity of drunken madness. His own entourage were no doubt writing into folklore his earlier chastisation of Flynn. The same devilish deed which led him to his predicament. The same entourage which he should have been in the middle of right now, conducting the orchestra. He managed to elevate himself the requisite few inches higher to grab a knee, he balanced himself on his patellar tendon as he pressed both hands against the cubicle wall for support. He managed to slowly pivot upwards, the increased elevation causing another series of retching. He took stock. Ross Marlowe, the alpha male hockey prodigy, was now standing here covered in vomit, excrement and God knows what else. How could he explain this? He couldn't face the proletariat like this. His ghostly appearance would be attributed to shitting his fuckin' pants. What is seen cannot be unseen. There was an exit door immediately after the hallway leading back into the bar. If he could make it down the hall without being spotted, he could duck out the door, glide down the steps and run like fuck till he got back to hockey rooms. It was dark outside, the only light was the illumination from inside the bar. All going well, he could get out of there undetected. His mind went into overdrive, the visualisation of getting back in the door of the hockey rooms, to sanctuary.

A flush of anxiety swept over him again, an aftershock. He felt his heart palpitating as a film of perspiration hugged his skin. He had become dehumanised. He took off his blazer and wrapped it up into a ball. He would use this as camouflage till he was clear of the steps, at which point he could dart diagonally across the cricket pitch, traverse the back of the rugby grounds and have less than two hundred metres before the refuge of the hockey rooms. Once he completed his mission unseen, he would call the family solicitor and all the powerful friends he knew. He would get the Gardaí. He would make sure Flynn was destroyed. If Flynn was living in a council house now, then he would make sure he was living on the streets and he wouldn't stop there. He would also hunt down his co-conspirator and ensure his ruination. All these thoughts of retribution abounded through Marlowe's head. His left hand glazed across his ear which renewed the claret trail of blood across his palm. This further heightened his siege mentality. His ignominious exit stirred even more rage inside him. The thoughts of his violation at the hands of the riff-raff sent him into a further wave of abhorrence.

Students came and went, oblivious to the fact that only yards away Marlowe was lying prostrate in a despicable mess. Through the door he had heard the interaction of his drunken peers as they engaged in micro conversations before heading back to the zoo inside the bar. Most of the conversations were one-liners about "Did you check out the rack of lamb on Sorcha?" "Great trout knocking about tonight" or "Some hoop on Aoife." One-liners which under normal circumstances would seem amusing but this was a code red emergency. Nothing else mattered except getting out of here unseen. Suddenly there was a hiatus in the noise, the main toilet door had closed and nobody re-entered. A window for escape. He opened the cubicle door and emerged onto the tiled floor. He caught sight of himself in the mirror which turned his stomach but he repelled the urge to vomit again and advanced onwards. The coast was clear to execute his evacuation. He had to get the fuck out of there now. He peered through a small opening in the main toilet door, the hallway was clear. His saturated beige cords and shirt inhibited his movement but this was a six-yard dash to freedom. Then it was only a matter of descending the steps and into the darkness, nobody would be the wiser. His non-slip sailor shoes would earn their corn here. He held his blazer tightly under his arm and made a bolt for freedom. He bounded down the hallway, meeting nobody on the way. Perfect. He briefly went from darkness to light as he grabbed the half moon door handle and pulled it open. Freedom was now within his grasp. He could see outside, the steps were clear and it was quiet, no impediment to his escape plan. Just as he stepped across the threshold, he felt two predatorial hands violently plunging into this shoulder blades. His worst nightmare was coming to pass. Flynn had assumed a stance only a few yards from the door in anticipation for Marlowe's great escape. Round One was to humiliate him privately but Round Two was the most important round of all, to humiliate him publicly. Marlowe caught a brief glimpse of himself in the window pane. His ghostly face of dread was accompanied by Flynn over his shoulder, looking like Beelzebub from the depths of hell. Flynn's eyes raged in an inferno. Marlowe's entourage were grouped at the corner of the bar across the wooden floor of the Pav. The perfect mini bowling lane of human skittles lined up perfectly. Psychotic energy coursed through Flynn's veins.

Vengeance electrified him. "No! Please, no!" Marlowe's last and final futile words before he became airborne. Flynn had used his powerful boot and almost superhuman strength to fire Marlowe across the room. As if shot out of a cannon, he soared towards his faithful entourage. His world stood still as he became airborne. Escape plan in tatters and his current predicament about to be exposed to his micro universe. A look of horror washed over the first of the faithful as he caught sight of his commander-in-chief hurtling towards them. All hell broke loose as the excrement-laden Marlowe crash-landed into the middle of his adoring entourage.

Flynn

The vivacious atmosphere was severed, screaming and the sound of glass breaking sent the decibel level into orbit. The impact and subsequent pandemonium resulted in four bodies laying strewn on the bar-room floor. Marlowe nestled at the bottom of this pile-up, almost concussed from another thunderbolt impact. The full attention of the revellers diverted to the scene of the mayhem. To the naked eye of the onlooker it was not entirely clear what exactly had transpired but as bodies gradually righted themselves they were exposed to the horror beneath. Through blurred vision, Marlowe could still make out the repulsive looks on the surrounding faces, oblivious to the horror he had been subjected to. His only instinct was to get as far away from this gathering as possible. Given the emanating stench from his saturated carcass he had best get going before he traumatised the onlookers even further. Marlowe peeled himself off the floor. "Get the fuck off me," he hollered to nobody in particular. He swung out wildly with an open-handed smack, inadvertently levelling one of his beloved entourage on the side of the head. That would be his final act, he turned and ran like a scalded hound, leaving his tie and blazer behind him. *Cinderella* had left the *Hockey Ball.*

Marlowe trundled down the outer steps, leapt over the black gate adjoining the cricket pitch and ran diagonally through the darkness. Some onlookers had poured outside to follow his get away. They looked on in bewilderment as the shadowy figure of Marlowe finally disappeared. There was a mixture of chuckles and horror from the masses gathered. A mixture of murmuring and disenchantment. The early postmortem was in full flow. "What the fuck happened him?" "Very un-Marlowe-like if you ask me," "Holy fuck, did Marlowe shit his pants?" asked another. Flynn and Hamish were among the revellers. Flynn took a long ponderous drag of his cigarette and grinned contently. The beast in his nature still very much at large. Hamish could no longer suppress the laughter and erupted in hyperventilated convulsions. How the tables had turned. "What has been seen cannot be unseen," said Flynn as he put his arm around Sophie and gestured her back to the bar, "three more creamy pints and make it three Sambucas as well please." There was an air of mystery around why Marlowe would hurl himself into his own faithful entourage covered in shite. Nobody witnessed Flynn's early assault on Marlowe and now it seemed his coup de grâce also went undetected. The barman slotted three Sambucas on the counter, oblivious to the recent conduct of the man they were serving. "Wow, I've no idea where I'll end up if I drink that!" said Sophie nervously surveying the Sambucas as Hamish added the finishing touches to each mini inferno, his hands still shaking involuntarily from his fit of giggling. "Trust me, what could possible go wrong," said Flynn with a devilish smile, "Viva la Revolución!"

Panicked and heavy breathing pierced the night air. Marlowe's chest felt heavy and his lungs burned with each step. He grunted loudly as he trundled forward about to blow a head gasket. The mixture of perspiration and Pav backwash bonded his shirt and beige cords to his skin. The foul stench suffocated the alveoli of his lungs. Each breath triggered a shooting pain in his chest and seemed to perforate his lungs. His breathing was becoming violently laboured as he ran full pelt around the bark mulch at the back of the rugby pitch. He assumed the day's alcohol consumption, attempted drowning, potential concussion and saturated clothing were sucking the life out of him. He persevered nonetheless and increased his pace even further. He was only the length of a cricket crease away from the cobble lock, from there he would only have another two hundred metres to the front door of his dorm. Marlowe felt a violent shudder which stopped him dead in his tracks. It was as if he had swallowed a hand grenade and it had just detonated inside his chest. He came to a complete halt beside the rugby scrum machine, a blue monstrosity which looked like an industrial road roller save for the cushion pads with giant "Rhino Rugby" cresting. He ran his fingers along the giant steel frame and felt the moisture of a few sporadic droplets from the nighttime condensation. He had seen the scrum machine being used numerous times by the formidable eight forwards for Trinity, who weighed just shy of a tonne. Their manic aggression could shunt this blue beast backwards with inhuman strength. But here was Marlowe, a capped hockey international, leaning against this machine for survival. A jolt of perspiration swept across his body as his lungs became starved of oxygen. A thunderbolt pain cut through his forehead and dizziness began to sweep over him. He could still hear the faint, far away din gently reverberating from the Pav. But he was in full darkness now and all alone along the shortcut. It was deadly quiet. Nobody would trespass here. He could see students walking along the cobble lock, illuminated by the famous Trinity lamps, only twenty metres away. He could call out and get help. He needed help, he needed to call for help. Marlowe was about to lose consciousness, he needed to cry out for help. A deep wheeze swept over him, it became constrictive.

Last chance. He decided to keep on moving. He was essentially holding his breath underwater, except there was no coming up for air. 'I can still make this' he told himself. Seconds left. Bang. He fell to his knees and neatly doubled over beside the scrum machine. His face nestled into the bark mulch. He involuntarily gave out a soft wheeze before becoming ever so still. The moon and stars shone brightly above his lifeless body.

Flynn

Chapter Seventeen: Friends

Brewster and Stokes had eyed Flynn from a distance all night long with a mild sense of malaise. Their intrigue was heightened by his interaction with Magnier, a native of exquisite bloodline and pedigree. Perhaps this character wasn't so bad after all. The arrival of his ginger-headed confrère added to their uneasiness, but neither were in the business of cowering to anyone. They resolved themselves to kick on with the festivities and thus far the night had gone swimmingly until the scandalous spectacle with Marlowe. An episode that served as a reminder of being ridiculed in public. The last thing they wanted was a confrontation with these two headbangers. They could see from their body language that they had little regard for their own personal well-being or those around them. Getting dragged into the bar fight and suffering a hiding would not enhance their reputation one iota. It felt like they were on safari, observing the wild animals from a distance. Rule number one on safari is not to approach the animals, but the intrigue was overwhelming. It was time they introduced themselves. Flynn watched as two blazers ventured towards them. He wondered if somehow word had filtered back to the high Chaparral about their earlier deeds. A showdown with club officers would certainly enhance the mayhem of the night but it would also sabotage any chance with Sophie. Flynn pulled Hamish close to him "Go easy here brother, I want to bag this bird," "Roger that, Captain Flynn," said Hamish with a grin. "Aye, Aye, Tigers," said Hamish as Brewster and Stokes approached. "Don't we know you from some place?" he paused and eyed up both of them in crazed fight poise. *'Ah for Jaysus sake,'* said Flynn to himself, he couldn't help but chuckle within, what a stupid move asking Hamish to play things cool! Hamish burst out laughing and grabbed the two of them in a giant bear hug. "Nice to meet you, Gents, I'm Hamish, this is Flynn and I think you already know the beautiful Sophie." Brewster returned the laughter albeit with slight reticence, "great to meet you guys, I'm Nick and this is Charlie," they exchanged handshakes. "You two lads were on fire last night in Judge Roy Beans, we were lucky to escape with our lives," said Stokes. *'Bingo!'* It was purely irrational rage, an extension of the madness. In fairness, they now stood before them with great magnanimity, no sense of ill will in the air. "Sure Jaysus, last night seems like a lifetime ago," said Flynn with a watery chuckle. "There's only one thing for it, five shots of Sambuca please, Barman!" He pirouetted and shouted in one perfect motion. Flynn may have been out of order but he wasn't going to apologize to anyone and heaven help them if they were holding out for one. Hamish beamed a smile as the five shots were racked up and he meticulously added the peace flame to each. "The answer to all of life's ills lies at the bottom of this liquorice paradise. Custer and Crazy Horse would have made friends if there was enough of this stuff around." They all laughed at the absurdity of Hamish's theatrics. "Let's make a toast to the Battle of Little Bighorn," roared Flynn, everyone joined in and toasted the same: "To the Battle of Little Bighorn!" Both Brewster and Stokes perceived a certain innocence behind the madness in Flynn and Hamish. The conversation and laughter trundled on uninhibited, perhaps they could get on after all. "Would you distinguished gentlemen fancy a bit of bag?" enquired Hamish with a beaming smile. "Sounds good," said Brewster without breaking stride. This wasn't their first dance with the devil. Flynn turned to Sophie, who was being swept along with the intoxicating adrenaline of the night. Flynn leaned forward and pulled her closer in intimate embrace, he could feel her perfume in his nostrils and that sweet scent of her skin, "Fancy a trip to the moon?" he whispered in her ear.

She pondered for a moment and then smiled in wholehearted accord, a trip to the moon sounded like a great idea. "Well, it is a full moon out tonight, be a shame to spoil it." She retained the closeness of their embrace and held Flynn close. He could feel her breath softly making landfall on his lips as an electric current of seduction swept through his body. Jackpot. His strong arms fully enveloped her perfectly chiselled frame and held her close as their mouths formed a perfect symmetry. She had fallen for his off-the-cuff madness, a temporary departure from her comfort zone of high achieving sports-people. He had fallen for her moon goddess features, her blinding beauty was hypnotic. After a few more seconds of trading deep-sea saliva, they gently detached, making sure to savour each parting drop. She smiled at Flynn and ran her tongue slowly across her upper lip with satisfaction. Flynn had suddenly garnered that x-factor magnetism. He glanced at Hamish, who was winking at him furiously in admiration whilst entertaining Brewster and Stokes. Hamish made the sign of a fist and mimicked a subtle sniff, it was time to crack on with their lunar adventure. "Our rocket ship awaits, my Lady!" said Flynn as he took her hand. Sophie accepted his palm and interlocked their fingers together, she looked glowingly into his eyes and brought their interlocking grip towards her perfect bosom. Flynn smiled back at her, the beast in his nature was bursting at the seams. He pulled her close again and kissed her neck, "this should be fun," he whispered. Hamish leaned in and put his arms around Brewster and Stokes, "start your engines and follow me, gentlemen." He pulled back the half-moon handle on the wooden exit door, "Cape Canaveral, this way!" They took an immediate left and ventured the few yards around to the secluded east wing viewing deck. Four large wooden picnic tables were empty and inviting. The wood on the tables was slightly splintered despite a fresh coat of varnish. They were either painted in a hurry or else the originator ran out of sand paper. They were the ideal student benches - indestructible. The area was also dimly lit and provided the perfect cover of darkness for their impending impropriety. Hamish jumped on top of the furthest picnic table and theatrically swung his arms around like a matador soaking up the fantasy adulation of a jam-packed Corrida. "Olé Torreros! Olé!" he roared as he unfurled another bulging plastic bag of his crystallised rocket fuel. He pursed his lips and neatly held his cigarette between his canine and lips. "Olé! Olé! Oh fuckin' Lé!" He set about his task with precision, the smouldering cigarette perched on his lips causing his eyes to water slightly. He meticulously began to formulate perfect rows across the cedar wood table making sure to centre each one with precision. Upon completion, he had ten perfectly constructed snow-white eskers spaced with geometric accuracy in front of the other four miscreants. "I'm loving your handy work here," said Brewster, "don't mind if I do," without hesitation he swooped downwards and hoovered up his allocated lines. "Oh yes baby!" as he recoiled in euphoria, "now that's good shit!" Hamish cut across him, "whatever happened to ladies first!" he grinned in the fading light, the ascension of cigarette smoke further obscuring his facial features - the devil incarnate. Flynn smiled as he emancipated his grasp from around Sophie's waist, he looked on as this beauty queen leaned forward and inhaled this pernicious white powder. The destruction of the soul. An equalizer. Flynn leant in beside her and blitzed his lines in a couple of seconds. He bolted upright with arms outstretched. "Viva la Revolución!" He retained his bind around Sophie as his arousal went into orbit, his mind flooded with thoughts of making passionate love. Stokes was the last member of the revellers to gild the lily. He beamed a giant smile as he felt the visceral invasion around his bloodstream, his eyes were entranced in a faraway gaze. The road to perdition had begun.

A new dynamic emerged as the five confrères bounded back into the Pav after the chemical baptism of their new friendship. There were no longer barriers between Flynn and the blazers. They were suddenly kindred spirits. Their hearts raced violently as the pristine white eskers rampaged through their bloodstreams and imbued them with invincibility. Brewster put his arm around Flynn's shoulder, a genuine show of camaraderie in the inebriated chaos. There was no longer a divisive trench of culture, money or status. They morphed into five unhinged students on high-grade cocaine having the time of their lives. Their inhibitions disappeared, Brewster and Stokes discarded the blazers as the next round of shots rolled and their body temperatures began to soar.

"Olé Torreros! Olé!" became the new war cry as shots fizzed down their throats. Stokes then bought a round of recently produced stimulant drink Red Bull which was relatively new on the market. "My cousin in San Diego tells me that Red Bull and vodka is the bomb! Apparently, Red Bull is derived from the adrenaline of fish as they suffocate on the shore after being caught. Just before their gill arch collapses they secrete this adrenaline solid and they melt it down, fizz it up and call it Red Bull."

Momentary wonder was followed by rapturous laughter. Stokes was on a roll. "There are health warnings about this Red Bull thing everywhere and yet it comes from the most beautiful marine life. Nearly everything they say is bad for you comes from nature. It doesn't make sense. For example, cocaine comes directly from Coca leaves, Fuckin' Coca leaves." Stokes had his gander up and was now firing on all cylinders, the others are struggling to contain their laughter but he's on fire. "The same Coca leaves that only grow for two months a year down in South American and the poor farmers actually pick them by hand. The poor bastards then have to mulch them down to make them into paste for resale. Now, fair enough they have to fuck in cement, gasoline, caustic soda and a rake of other shite but it's hard work and it comes from the land!" Cue a Mount Vesuvius eruption of laughter.

Flynn sparked up another cigarette, one arm around Brewster and another around Sophie. The blazer and the beauty, a long way from the anxiety ridden mess who darkened the Front Arch. Flynn broke his bind from Brewster to pick up his vodka and Red Bull, the ice-cold contents precipitating molecules of condensation which ran down into the palm of his hand. He ran his thumb across the micro droplets as he reflected on the death of Daryl Flynn, the real-life exorcism, the liberation and rebirth he was now experiencing. He didn't give a fuck that his soft inner nature had been ripped apart and replaced by the beast. He embraced this phenomenon. His Edward Hyde had slain his Henry Jekyll, and now only Hyde remained. "To immortality! He roared as he raised his glass and beckoned everyone to follow suit. He chugged back the contents and slammed his glass back down on the counter and beckoned the barman for another round. He looked at Sophie, his eyes bulging widely with arousal. She held his gaze, she returned his telepathy as the wildness in their eyes locked together. Soon their inner beasts would meet.

Flynn

Chapter Eighteen: Sophie

Hamish reckoned he was 'on a promise' with Sarah down in Charlotte Quay, so they temporarily parted ways. He gave Flynn a bag of coke and the keys to his dorms. "Now that's what real friends are for!" as he erupted into a convulsion of Hamish laughter. The short walk from the Pav to the dorms would take almost an hour. Every few yards Flynn and Sophie would re-engage their lips in passionate symmetry. They stopped at almost every dimly lit campus lantern to renew their romance. One such campus lantern adorned the top corner of the rugby pitch. It was there they stopped for a prolonged hiatus. It was one of the darkest and most intimate spots on the walk back. They kissed passionately under the moonlight, carefree and high, enjoying every ounce of sensual pleasure. Flynn stood on the bark mulch with his back against the railings, he interlocked both hands as he pulled Sophie close in perfect embrace, he felt the full curvature of her body against his. Sophie felt safe in his arms, she felt an honesty of spirit within him. He was non-conformist and aloof yet confident in his own skin. It was that kiss where she felt a love and trust growing inside her. The campus was deadly quiet. The air perforated only by the gentle sound of saliva being exchanged between their lips and their feverish breathing. Geographically they were in the heart of Dublin city centre but metaphysically they had inhabited a new planet of which they had sole residency. The moon shone brightly above them and illuminated their lustful zest. Unbeknownst to them, only twenty yards away the same moon also shone brightly on Marlowe's lifeless body. The moment was further enchanting their body impulses. Flynn ran his hands lower towards Sophie's knee and slowly scrolled upwards along her thigh.

Flynn

The sound of her breathing elevated as Flynn's hand reached the border of skin and laced G-string. His ran his hand upwards across the bristly lace till his hand felt her lower abdomen. He gently used his thumb to climb over the coarse ridge and smoothly began the downwards descent. Sophie hissed an "Ooooh Yes" in his ear. Her G-string was now down to her lower thighs as Flynn's hand made the ascent back upwards, slowly and purposely. Sophie groaned with exhilaration and kissed Flynn even more deeply. Suddenly they heard a cacophony of noise at the far end of the pitch. It was a gang of jocks 'off their heads' after a barnstormer of a drinking session in rugby rooms. They were now out on the field throwing a rugby ball around in the dark and shrieking hysterically. The perfect mood killer. "To be continued…" said Sophie seductively as she fixed herself back up, "we have a date with destiny."

They giggled together, the laughter that only a couple in lustful trance can jointly assimilate. They passed by the front of the Berkeley library, pausing again beside the giant gold-plated globe for another prolonged embrace. It was there that they heard the decibel levels of the rugby drunks go into orbit, they were properly going off on one. "Those boys must be on some heavy gear," said Flynn with a smile, "seems I'm not the only Werewolf that this full moon brought out tonight." Every step, every touch, every taste of saliva was reverberating through the senses. They kept walking till finally they reached the dorm entrance, their final destination on their amorous voyage. Flynn pulled open the heavy wooden door with his left hand, "home sweet home, let's make it all the sweeter," another kiss heightened their passion even further. The feral nature of lust inside themselves reaching its zenith. With the door, half ajar he used his full frame to hold it open as they kissed passionately under the moonlight. "Let's do it here," whispered Sophie as she ran her hands up Flynn's chest. She began to undo his belt buckle as the sound of a siren rippled through the air. They burst out laughing again, Flynn looked at her and touched her lips with his right hand, "let's get you inside, no more interruptions," he ushered Sophie inside. Flynn could see the reflection of the flashing lights at the far end of campus as he closed the door behind him. *'Those gobshites must really be running a muck over there,'* he thought to himself. "The stairwell to heaven," said Sophie as she interlocked her fingers in Flynn's once again. Flynn surveyed the surroundings of this perfectly preserved Georgian architecture. He thought about the good and the great that passed through these hallowed dorms for centuries. The only surviving witnesses were these immense walls which still stared back at them. He wondered if these walls had ever seen someone punching so far above his weight as he was now. Flynn paused momentarily and opened up his body to take in the awe of the Georgian surroundings. Sophie paused in unison, she was on the step above him and rested her head on his shoulder. Flynn began with great gusto, "these walls have stood for hundreds of years and witnessed thousands of students coming through its bowels. The great and the good have gone to Trinity but I can guarantee you this, these walls have never ever seen anything as beautiful as you." He turned and kissed Sophie with raw passion. This enchanting monologue was delivered contritely and from the heart. He never hesitated or broke stride, it was romantic, seductive and laced with adoration. Sophie felt Flynn's love permeate the walls of her heart. Their drug-induced state convinced them both of their everlasting love. Flynn had the perfect predatorial intuition of elevating the emotional stakes before potential intercourse. It was no longer about preying on the weak, it was now about preying on the strong by finding their weakness. Sophie was deluded by the transience of their love, her intoxicating high made her even more vulnerable to Flynn's advances. Powerless to resist. "I agree, and that's why, Mister Flynn, tonight we will be making our own bit of history, make sure these walls have something to talk about." Sophie left her tongue out to personify her impending promiscuity. Flynn opened the dorm room door, the beast in his nature was primed. They were finally alone and wouldn't be disturbed.

Sophie laid back on the dorm room table exposing her tanned and perfectly chiselled abdomen. The flawless curvature of her abdomen muscles oscillating ever so slightly as she giggled and tried to suppress her laughter. Flynn leaned forward and snorted a giant line of cocaine from beside her belly button. He recoiled as the white turbo force hit his bloodstream. After a brief electric shock to the senses, he leaned back in and kissed Sophie. She put both arms around his neck and pulled him towards her. Their drug-induced tactility accelerating a matrimony of arousal. The all-night drinking coupled with their recent ascension was the perfect concoction. Flynn felt the expedition of blood flow around his body. He felt invincible and with every passing second, he felt more and more confident about having a girl of this calibre in his arms. He pulled his now 'signature' Clockwork Orange t-shirt over his head, exposing his bare chest. Sophie ran her hands from his neck down his pecks and all the way to his belt buckle. Flynn pulled her back towards the couch, she slowly peeled her top off and momentarily paused to run her fingers down her sides. Her intense kisses letting him know that she wanted every ounce of this. Their bodies pulled together, that first sensation of flesh upon flesh. She undid Flynn's belt buckle as he gyrated upwards and allowed room to pull down his jeans. His erection reached its zenith upon liberation. Sophie smiled admiringly as she took custody of his erection in her right hand. She stood back and pulled down her skirt. Flynn lay back on the couch to watch the magnificence of her full unveiling. She paused for a moment to allow him to absorb her full beauty before re-engaging. A gentle spiral of perspiration came over Flynn as she gently straddled him again. Utopia. The feeling of insertion was not only physical, it catapulted his mind into a different stratosphere of happiness. He visualised Sophie in the Pav at that moment when he first caught sight of her as he salivated over her beauty. That same beauty was now naked and making love to him. Her breathing rhythmically increased as her pleasure hormones went into orbit. Both were brought to almost synchronised climax. Sophie lay down on top of Flynn as he remained inside her. Flynn ran his hands down the perfect curvature of her spine as a small sliver of sweat beaded in his fingers. They kissed some more as Flynn glanced at the table, another plentiful supply of cocaine remained. A giant smile illuminated his face, "the best is yet to come."

Flynn

Chapter Nineteen: Garryowen

A giant Garryowen was hoofed in the air as a drunken pack of prairie dogs ran full belt in pursuit, "Catch it, Chasers!" roared Crotty followed by hysterical laughter. Crotty was the supremely gifted out-half and captain of the Trinity first team. He had already written his name into folklore by dragging a mediocre outfit through three consecutive promotions from division four to division one - the promised land. The 'elite' rugby squad had a 'team bonding night' which had been celebrated in the rugby dressing rooms situated in the bowels of the Pav. Rugby bonding nights were messy affairs at the best of times but the Freshers' week bash was the blue riband of messy nights, complete with initiations and kangaroo-court punishments. It was a fully-blazered affair and attendees were fully decked out in crested ties and jackets. The only difference between the rugby posse and their hockey brethren was sheer size. The rugby lads were giants, the depth of their blazers akin to scaffolding catch nets on small buildings. This year the chosen poison of punishment was Jägermeister mixed with crème de menthe, the perfect potion to awaken the Frankenstein in everyone. After hours of mayhem there had finally been an adjournment to proceedings and the dogs of war had now spilled over to College Park, the hallowed turf of the rugby empire. Crotty's giant Garryowen came out of the sky like a meteor crashing down to earth, Dominic Saint George was under the ball, or so he thought. Between the dark sky and the impairment from Jägermeister and Crème de menthe, he never stood a chance. It was brilliance in itself to be in the vicinity of the dropping ball. He tilted his head back towards the moonlit sky in great expectation but suddenly he couldn't see a thing.

His next sensation was the ball smashing him straight between the eyes on the upper bridge of his nose. His comrades collapsed in convulsions of laughter, their impeccable dress attire sabotaged as they rolled around the turf in uncontrollable hysteria. Saint George laughed as loud as any of the platoon, he touched his face and felt a trickle of claret coming down his nostril which heightened the humour even more. Crotty retrieved the ball and starting spinning a few passes out wide as they advanced up the field in a pre-rehearsed yet drunkenly executed move. All designed to give Crotty a shot at a drop goal from just outside the phantom opposition 22-yard line. Their delirium burned brightly and the laughter lit up the night. It now moved on to the final coup de grâce, a snap pass from scrum-half, Curneen, purely reliant on telepathy given the darkness and his obscene drunkenness. He had at this stage unbuttoned his blazer to liberate his shoulders, his non-slip sailor shoes offered no traction on the dew-laden grass but this was a must. Despite the elements, he managed to whip the perfect pass back into the breadbasket of Crotty. A film of moisture now gripped the ball but Crotty spidered all ten fingers around the dimpled oval leather. He stole one quick glance at the posts and then Boom! He kicked a 'beezer,' straight out of the meat. The ball took off into campus orbit but just as it reached cruising altitude it ricocheted off the right-hand post and spun wide. The laughter erupted as they converged on Crotty. Drunken horseplay. The gigantic forwards playfully mauled him on the ground, punishment beating for his miss. A physical violation that only rugby teammates could reconcile. To the average person, it would be considered grievous bodily harm but Crotty laughed it off. In the midst of the madness there was a shrieking cry of terror.

Flynn

Curneen had resolved himself to retrieve the rugby ball after Crotty's bazooka cannoned off the post. It was also safer to follow the ball. As Crotty's half-back partner, he could be in line for a similar 'hiding' by association. He jogged underneath the posts, sniggering to himself as his comrade got his comeuppance back at the 22. He spotted the ball over by the scrum machine and transitioned from the grass to the bark mulch. It was the perfect night. What an absolute barnstormer of a bonding session, a lot of similarly minded lads on the same page. Positive vibes ahead of a big season ahead. The moonlight reflected off the giant steel cylinders. He felt a sudden jolt of uneasiness. A tsunami of anxiety and dizziness came over him. His spine tingled and a sweat perforated his shirt. Sobriety hit like a right hook to the jaw. His pace slowed. Each step across the bark mulch became more contrived. Beads of sweat formed on his eyelids. 'Cop the fuck on Curneen,' he grinned to himself with false reassurance. He had kicked balls over and back on the College Park pitches thousands of times and knew every blade of glass. There was something wrong. His sickening feeling confirmed that, the feral instinct when the human body senses that death is close by. At first sight it looked as if someone had dumped a couple of tackle bags and coverings beside the scrum machine. He got closer and his eyes adjusted to perfect probing focus. Whatever was on the ground wasn't tackle bags. His insides somersaulted. An army of sweat molecules marched over his skin.

The body of Ross Marlowe lay face down and lifeless before him. The raucousness of his comrades flatlined as a micro silence descended. Curneen knelt to the ground and gently rolled Marlowe onto his side. Marlowe's eyes were still wide open, both his hands clenched in fists full of bark mulch. His last act on the planet as he searched in vain for a pocket of oxygen. The events of the night had triggered lung trauma which precipitated a giant asthma attack and ultimate cardiac arrest. Curneen's stomach revolted, morphed from concave to convex as the full contents evacuated in one violent retch. He collapsed against the scrum machine and turned back to cry out but the shock had temporarily strangled his vocal cords. He heard more laughter from the posse as one of them shouted, "Curneen! You better not be getting sick on that scrum machine or you'll be licking it off next Tuesday." The constricted airflow and vocal paralysis slightly subsided as he managed to intonate a muffled cry of "Get Help…" but this came out as a whisper and barely audible. He looked back down at the cadaver, this was no time to freeze. He became unshackled as he rose up to his full height and unleashed the zenith of his vocal cords. His lungs exploded in volcanic eruption, "GET HELP! GET HELP! GET FUCKIN' HELP" He slumped back on the scrum machine and sunk to the ground, he put an arm across Marlowe.

The cavalry arrived in seconds, the horror in Curneen's voice had severed the party atmosphere. "Anyone got a phone on them?" gasped Curneen with a husky wheeze seeping through his voice. "I have but I've no credit" replied Dominic Saint George recoiling from the shock before him. "Ye don't need fuckin' credit, Dom, just dial 999 for fuck sake!" his voice exploding with urgency. Crotty leaned across Marlowe, checked his breathing and for signs of a pulse. "Holy Fuck Guys, this is Ross Marlowe!" Crotty shouted as the enormity of the discovery began to take hold of him. Curneen rolled Marlowe on the flat of his back as Crotty commenced chest compressions, "We need to fuckin' try" his voice tailing off with raw emotion. "Yes, hello," Saint George breathed deeply, emotion began to take over, "We've found someone, eh I think his name is Ross Marlowe, he's… he's not breathing… And eh, he has no… he has no pulse." His breathing oscillated. "We're in College Park in Trinity campus, we need help." The operator asked him to stay on the line as they talked him through CPR while the ambulance was en route. One of the lads ran back towards the Pav shouting wildly and trying to summon help. Crotty violently plunged both hands downwards on Marlowe's ribcage as he tried, in vain, to resuscitate him. By the time the ambulance came careering through the Nassau Street gate, he couldn't feel his hands any more. He was pulverizing Marlowe's chest. He could hear bones cracking, but no life. The soul had left his body. The paramedics wasted no time rigging the defibrillator cords to Marlowe's body. They administered three separate shocks before loading him onto a stretcher and into the ambulance. They proceeded to resuscitation phase two as they injected adrenaline into his blood stream. Marlowe's body was still lifeless. Both paramedics looked at each other, that familiar look, no dialogue required. Their training commanded them to keep working. As per the life-saving handbook, they sped off to the hospital in the hope of a miracle. Marlowe was pronounced dead upon arrival. The King of Irish Hockey, the man who commanded an audience everywhere he went, the man to whom life came so easily, had now flatlined on the electrocardiogram. His lifeless body lay there covered in vomit, excrement and bark mulch chipping. Death - the great equaliser. The personification of the fragility of life.

It had been bright for several hours. Flynn and Sophie were still wild-eyed but the bag of cocaine had finally been vanquished. They were now on the way down from the summit. Physically and mentally, they had exhausted every sinew of their bodies. "I never want to go back to the girl I was," said Sophie. She had just finished a complex dialogue about losing friends over infatuations with ex-boyfriends. Their naked bodies encased each other as they bound together. Sophie lay back across Flynn's chest as he cradled her in his arms. Thick cigarette smoke enveloped the dorm.

Since their arrival back at the dorm they had developed the perfect circle of love. The sequence was to have sex, smoke a cigarette, talk about their inner demons, have a line of cocaine, have sex and repeat the process. The lack of cocaine now disrupted the supply chain, so they were stuck on the inner demons' conversation. It had been bright for several hours and their gruelling routine required a ceasefire. Both finally began to drift off to sleep, the restless beasts in their nature finally granting a small reprieve. Flynn drifted off into a restful paradise. His sensory neurons now resided in heaven as he held Sophie in his arms and closed his eyes. He had tasted manna from the Gods. His inner beast had brought him to a new frontier, a frontier of happiness where he could taste and smell happiness. This was only the start he said to himself as he transitioned into dreamland.

The brief sojourn didn't last long. He was awoken by his sixth sense, a feeling that someone else was in the room, part of mankind's feral protection instinct. He realised he had to wake but had not yet reached the land of consciousness. Sophie was still wrapped in his arms but he felt a presence lingering over them, that subtle body heat and breath. He heard a familiar voice, "Matey, wake up, I've got some news." Hamish's large hand touched his shoulder. "Come on, Matey." Flynn opened his eyes, his vision was dogged by the joint collaboration of the smoke-filled room and the gestation of toxins inside his body. Hamish looked at Sophie, who was still happily residing in dreamland. He looked at Flynn, "Matey, what a score! She is world-class trout!" he whispered through a smile, "but something mad has happened, we need to talk."

Hamish flashed him a psychotic smile. Flynn prised himself slowly from the naked body of Sophie. A departure from Utopia. She didn't wake, a beautiful pose of beauty as she slept in nature. Hamish couldn't resist an opportunistic perv before Flynn pulled the covers back over her. "Matey! She is a fuckin' ten! She's a unicorn brother. Such specimens only exist when we die and go to some place up North," Hamish whispered through suppressed excitement. Flynn beamed a yawning smile as he followed Hamish into the kitchen. He was sexed out and drugged out. For now. "What fuckin' time is it brother?" said Flynn, he knew it has been bright for several hours. "It's ten bells, the early birds catch all the worms," grinned Hamish. "That may be true," said Flynn, "but don't forget it's the second mouse that gets the cheese." Flynn closed the kitchen door so as not to disturb Sophie. "So what's the fuckin' news?" asked Flynn returning to a semi composed state. Flynn stood in his boxers, leaning back against the cramped student kitchen. The hobs had suffered corrosion over time from the overuse of student culinary delights, baked beans and burnt rashers. A toaster lay in the corner which looked like it still retained the burnt flakes of bread of the past fifty years. Hamish still looked immaculate. Silk shirt and cravat. The slightly bloodshot eyes and stubble were the only outliers to betray the look of a man who may have just as easily had a quiet night in, drinking tea. "Fuckin' hell, Matey, that Sarah is a wild one." He unbuttoned the top three buttons of his shirt and unveiled his left shoulder blade which was covered in bloodied and deep lacerations. "Holy Jaysus!" said Flynn, did you shack up with a Bengali Tiger for the fuckin' night?" Cue more laughter. "Oh she's a rare one alright!" Hamish handed him a cigarette which Flynn greatly accepted, the laughter finally subsided.

"So Matey, a bit of a news bulletin in no particular order, our old pal Marlowe is dead, apparently found by the Rugby stunt-dogs in the bark mulch in College Park and also according to Robin, my roommate from downstairs, your sister rang several times after you sent that text. Apparently some bird called Rachel killed herself, reckoned you knew her well, funeral is on later this afternoon, herself and your Mum are worried about you, want you to go home straight away and all that palaver." Hamish took a long drag of his cigarette and exhaled as if he was after reading out the contents of a shopping list. "Any of those stories take your fancy?" asked Hamish, as if enquiring whether he wanted soft or hard-boiled eggs for breakfast.

Flynn stared at the flaking paint on the wall and took a drag from his cigarette. He exhaled slowly, curved his lips and slowly intonated the word "Fuck" as he maintained his gaze on the wall. The shocking news stirred something deep inside him. Momentarily, the original Daryl Flynn resurfaced in his soul. A resurrection of inconvenience. A wave of desolation and hurt pierced his gut. What had he become? *'Why the fuck am I in the kitchen across from this maniac, drugged to the gills and smoking a cigarette as Hamish brazenly and apathetically recounts two deaths?'* The thoughts of his last interactions with Rachel came flooding back. She had adored him. Most of all, she had respected him, always saw the best in him. She wanted to bring him out of the shadows. He had told her he loved her. *'I looked her in the eyes and told her I loved her!'* And all to coerce her into sex. *'I manipulated her fragile emotions. I made her feel like someone really cared and then never answered her calls or texts again. She was from a tough home but she was humble and most of all she was fuckin' nice. And kind-hearted. I blanked her forever. Now she's dead.'*

Questions bamboozled his thought process, *'did she think of me while she walked to her death? Oh, fuck Flynn, what have you done.'* Just then a stabbing pain punctured Flynn's sternum. His lungs began to cease functioning and his face turned bright red. A bead of sweat broke across his brow. His thoughts became further entrenched. *'And what of Marlowe, a lesson in respect through humiliation?'* The grievous assault in the toilets boomed through his brain. He was drunk and brash but typical of the self-righteous class of the Trinity glitterati. *'Overdue a slap, but no more.'* The vision of him struggling as he drowned in the toilet bowl came bounding across his senses, violently gripping his thigh as he speared him downwards. *'And the look in Marlowe's eyes. Desperation.'* The thoughts of his impending mortality banishing any thoughts of grandeur. He may have worn a blazer into the Pav but his quest for survival was the same as anyone. *'Strip it all back and we are all the same. We arrive into the world with nothing and leave this world with nothing.'*

His eyes began to well up. His heart filled with sadness and remorse. The vulnerability of two days ago when he met "science-girl" in Front Square came flooding back. He felt awkward and his legs began to tremble. That horrible dizziness swept over him. His heart began palpitating and anxiety infiltrated his bloodstream. He suddenly reflected on his transformation into this monster. It wasn't just over the past forty-eight hours but had festered long before that. The beast had laid dormant. There was a breaking point. A trigger. He gasped for air and bent over. Panic was setting in, he needed to breathe. Hamish looked across the kitchen at him in bewilderment, "You alright, Matey? No point crying over spilt milk now!" Flynn hyperventilated and gasped, the lung constriction forced a shuddering pain which reverberated in his head. *'I can't breathe.'*

He looked at the floor and felt himself losing consciousness, when suddenly he felt a giant inflation of his lungs which bolted him upright. He sprang back against the rinky-dink kitchen cabinets and stood upright. His muscles began to clench and his heart started to resupply his capillaries with oxygen. The anxiety, guilt, sadness and desolation evaporated from his heart. The beast had awoken and once again commanded the battleship. It was Daryl Flynn's final roll of the dice. Having re-emerged from the deep and made it back to the surface, he now disappeared back into the depths below. And this time deeper towards the ocean floor. The temporary transition was shattered, now the beast in his nature roared back. *'How the fuck could you allow that fuckin' loser back into your thoughts?'* Visions of the madness and mayhem of the past forty-eight hours flooded this mind, but this time he reacted to each thought with golden admiration. Every millisecond of chaos at breakneck speed. This time there was no recrimination or guilt, only adulation at how far he had travelled from the shell of Daryl Flynn. He stood up to his full towering height and flicked his shoulders backwards. A sadistic grin crossed his face. "Sure, ye can't make an omelette without breaking a few fuckin' eggs!" This elicited a barking laugh from Hamish as he bent over and exhaled a chuckle. "And by the way, have you any bag left?" enquired Flynn. "I most certainly do, Matey, I most certainly do…" Hamish lined up another couple of snow-white eskers on the battered wooden table. "Breakfast of Champions." Flynn recoiled slowly from this latest hit. A giant smile pierced the corners of his mouth as the whites of his eyes turned ruby red. "Ye know, Matey… I've got a beautiful feeling about today." Flynn looked at Hamish, their eyes met. A chaotic telepathy. Hamish reciprocated a smile, "so do I, Matey… So do I!" Flynn slowly sparked up a cigarette and inhaled ponderously. Dark thoughts flooded his mind. It felt as if he was plunging into the darkest and scariest depths of his own soul. Visualisations of mayhem infiltrated his thoughts.

Vengeance.

"I think it's time to settle some old scores…" All the years of violent daydreaming came shuddering into his consciousness. All the years he stared at the Uma Thurman poster fantasising about retribution. Retribution against those who made him feel like he did. All those people who made Daryl Flynn the fucked-up loser he was. Flynn looked out the window, the smile further broadened across his face.

"So much to do and so little time…"

Flynn

Chapter Twenty: The Righteous Man

The bedside alarm clock brought a shuddering halt to a particularly lucid and pleasurable dream. The first few seconds of bliss rudely interrupted by the realisation that work beckoned once again. Frank pawed a half comatose arm towards the snooze button. "Ah bollix anyway," he whispered. He rolled over and tried to re-enter the dream portal but to no avail. He wiped a crusted layer of drool from this chin as his tongue tried to reintroduce moisture around his mouth. The night before he had replicated his usual routine. After knocking off in the Watermill, he had gone to the Cedar Lounge for a few late drinks. The remnants of his overnight dehydration had now crystallized on his chin. He stared at the ceiling and exhaled loudly. Today he's on the early shift opening up the Watermill, he would be on his own. He visualises the day ahead and grimaces. His plans had seen scuppered by the impending funeral that afternoon. All things being equal, he would have easily coerced Alice Flynn into a hook-up. An afternoon booty call. A soft target for his charms. But not today. He would have to pass the hours till the evening without any lustful hiatus.

He dragged his rotten carcass out of bed in preparation for the usual morning ritual. Two boiled eggs, two coffees and a walk with the dog. He limped downstairs and tried to recalibrate sobriety with each step. He put on the kettle before pouring himself a large glass of orange juice. The ice-cold syrup flowed sharply down this gullet which caused him to shudder. "Jaysus that hit the spot alright," he whispered as each drop seemed to counteract the sugar low from last night's revelry. He rattled around the press and emerged with a saucepan. The coronation of the two boiled eggs was underway. He sauntered out to the hall and caught a glimpse of himself in the mirror. He paused and maintained eye contact with himself. He never started out to have an affair. It had been put on plate for him. Married for twenty-two years. Happily married. Curiosity had got the better of him. And now here he was, no intention of leaving his wife, but no intention of foregoing the odd hook up. A match made in heaven. Guilt consumed him at the beginning but after a while it became part of his routine. He was quiet. Kept himself to himself. He thought about ending it numerous times but it was too easy, too convenient. Gratification was king. He was weak, but she was even weaker. Alice was bound by a vow of omertà. She had no real friends and both her kids were like ghosts. She often talked about their issues and how they hugged the shadows. Pillow talk. He cared, he truly did but he was already a father and a husband. This was no time to put his head above the parapet. He enjoyed his low profile and that's the way it would stay. He got changed and went about his business.

The village was quiet as he made the short walk down to the Watermill. He had worked there for fifteen years. Another marriage of convenience. The regulars knew him and he knew them. The perfect comfort zone. He worked three 'earlies' a week and enjoyed the solitude. The brief hiatus of the calm before the regulars began their descent through the doors. He was routine-driven and highly efficient. On the morning in question, he went about his business as usual, whistling with abandon and prepping for the first regular through the doors. It was customary to leave the front door open for ventilation. All was now in order. After a brief sojourn in the keg room, he ventured back up the stairs. He paused upon reentry. The scent of fresh cigarette smoke hit his lungs.

He wasn't alone…

Hours earlier, Flynn had retraced his footsteps back to the family home. Where it all began. The humble surrounds of his Artane council house. It felt as if he was inhabiting the world of someone he no longer knew. The artist formerly known as Daryl Flynn was no more. His head had been severed and his blood had flowed across the Trinity campanile. The raging beast inside was now laid bare. He stopped at the entrance and allowed himself a giant smile. 'Home sweet home.' He sparked up a cigarette and ventured onwards. The echo of the side lane triggered another smile. It was a homecoming unlike no other. Daryl Flynn by name only. He pushed open the back door. His sister Vanessa and his mother sat in an uneasy silence around the table. His previous hatred and contempt for them was now replaced by amusement.

"Good morning ladies" he bellowed and exhaled a giant plume of smoke. "Grey day out there for a funeral. Tragic about poor Rachel. The wheels just seemed to come off the wagon at the wrong time. Let's just hope she's in a better place now… Nobody should suffer on like that… eh? Would either of you mind sticking me on a bacon sambo? I'm famished and badly in need of a shower."

He skipped across the kitchen floor and rustled his sister's hair before disappearing down the hall. They looked across the table at each other in momentary silence. Vanessa swallowed deeply, "Daryl… Eh, Daryl!" her facial features contorted as she tried to reconcile the force of nature which had bounded across the floor with her conflicted and self-loathing brother.

"Are you OK, Daryl?" Flynn paused and bent his head back around the corner. "Never better sis, never better," he flashed her a wink and clicked his tongue. "Now, giddy up, we've a funeral to go to and then I've got to be back into town to meet some friends. Give the grill a good rattle!" His mother had long since given up on building emotional bridges with her son. Her vocal cords still hadn't reacted to the unveiling of whatever had just walked in the door, puffing on a cigarette. She cleared her throat, "Daryl!" she called, "eh, Daryl, can you come here please… Daryl!" Silence. The squeaking of the shower faucet was the only retort as water gushed on the faux granite of the shower floor. The conversation would have to wait. In fact, her beckoning would remain unanswered…

The flick of the flint wheel of a lighter broke the deathly silence in the Watermill as an elongated inhalation crunched through the cigarette paper. Flynn nestled back and exhaled slowly. He flicked the overhanging ash into the ashtray in front of him and took in the eerie silence. Mindfulness. Frank had developed a gift of looking at people whilst still seemingly maintaining a downward gaze at the ground. "I think I know yer man," he murmured to himself, "defo looks familiar, not a regular but must be a local, defo seen him before…"

Three days of beard stubble camouflaged Flynn even further. Frank cast a quick glance at his watch. '*Not quite time for opening but sure not far off.*' He noted that the front door had now been closed. He theorised that the conscientious early morning customer had closed it behind him to keep the draft out. Frank strode purposely towards the centre of the bar. All things considered, he was in good form. "Howya, Bud, you're an eager beaver this morning… what can I get ye?" Frank rested his hands on the beer taps in preparation. Flynn smiled at his familiarity. "Good morning, Matey, beautiful day out there, could you stick me on a creamy pint of stout please?" Frank flipped down the Guinness tap, the pressurised nitrogen emitting the unmistakable hiss as the black velvet made love to a fresh glass. Flynn closed his eyes. He breathed gently in through his nose and gently out through his mouth as he listened to the sound which enlivened his senses, the sound of a first creamy pint coming his way.

"Awful tragedy for the parish," said Frank as he put the pint down in front of Flynn and leaned across the counter. "Poor girl had her whole life ahead of her, you'd wonder how someone could do that to themselves." He was visibly contrite. Flynn picked up the pint and smiled. He lowered down over half the contents and exhaled with gratification. He repeated the words Frank had just uttered: "whole life ahead of her…" He paused and looked at Frank. "And what age are you, Matey?" he hissed in a sinister tone. Frank engaged the question despite the intrusive nature, "Jaysus would ye believe I'm turning fifty in a few days, have an auld bash planned for Saturday night down in Raheny GAA club, the family have sorted the whole thing, will be a proper blow out, sure jaysus ye only live once… ye only get one bite of the cherry." Frank mobbed the counter with a smile.

Flynn flashed him another smile and licked the cream from his top lip. "Matey, did ye ever see Pulp Fiction?" he enquired through a casual exhalation of his cigarette. Frank looked at him with incredulity, '*something not quite right with this young fella,*' he thought to himself. "Eh, no I haven't, why you ask that?" He retorted, quietly perturbed. Flynn glared at him with an icy, psychotic stare, "I'll tell ye why, there's a line in it that goes as follows…"

Flynn got to this, feet and transitioned into his scariest Samuel L. Jackson pose; "The path of the righteous man is beset on all sides by the inequities of the selfish and the tyranny of evil men. Blessed is he who, in the name of charity and good will, shepherds the weak through the valley of darkness, for he is truly his brother's keeper and the finder of lost children. And I will strike down upon thee with great vengeance and furious anger, those who would attempt to poison and destroy My brothers. And you will know My name is the Lord when I lay My vengeance upon thee."

Flynn raised his voice for the crescendo and smashed a fist down on the bar counter. "I bet ye thought you'd never see me again, Frank?" Flynn's eyes narrowed as he looked at him in a death stare. "Eh… how the fuck do ye know my name, pal?" Frank felt a flood of anxiety wash over him. They were on their own in the bar. Frank then realised why the door was closed. Flynn looked familiar. '*But was he…?*'

Just as the epiphany was about to register, Flynn sprang over the counter and smashed both fists into either side of Frank's head, a thunderclap. Frank's senses became temporarily nullified as Flynn gripped him around the neck and smashed his head into the bar counter. The sickening thud was like a stun grenade. "Now, Sweetheart, no good deed goes unpunished… You've been a bold boy, Frank."

Flynn arched himself over the counter and waited for Frank to regain his senses. He locked his left hand underneath Frank's collar and raised him back up to eye level. Their faces were now only inches apart. Frank began his ascent back into consciousness. The blurred image of Flynn mutated and flickered as his eyes continued to betray him. Flynn held his blinkering gaze and returned a leering smile. Frank felt warm claret flow from his nose into his mouth. His breathing became laboured. "You're… You're Alice Flynn's young fella? Now wait, son… Please. I can help ye… Just ease up a minute. Please…" He looked into Flynn's eyes. There would be no mercy.

"Last bite of the cherry, Frank!" Flynn flashed him another smile. It was time to fight back. Frank sank a right hook into Flynn's jaw. It landed flush but served only as token resistance. "Now that's the spirit, soldier!" barked Flynn as he barrelled into a cacophony of laughter. He still had the commanding position over Frank. "Any last thoughts, sweetheart? Send me a postcard from the abyss." Frank cocked his fist and readied himself for one final counter assault. His innate survival instinct decreed that the fight must go on. He grunted and began swinging wildly. Flynn roared encouragement as Frank vainly rained blows across the counter. Each one was met with thunderous laughter. Frank began to punch himself out as hyperventilation took hold. "Party's over, Frank!" The smile on Flynn's face morphed into a psychotic grimace. "Boom!" Flynn brought down the guillotine. He cupped his hands around Frank's neck and reacquainted his face with the bar counter. The violent thud robbed Frank of his consciousness. Six more violent smashes followed. Each one with even greater ferocity before mercy would finally be granted. "Filthy fuckin' animal!" roared Flynn, the veins in his neck bulging as he pierced the decibel level. Flynn slumped back down on his bar stool and exhaled. "Happy birthday, sweetheart! Me fuckin' Ma says hello! Don't forget to take a good bite out of that cherry!" Blood splattered across the bar counter. A slippery resin inculcated the exterior of his perfect pint. Red speckles floated on the creamy head. Frank lay motionless across the counter, Flynn still held him tightly with his left hand, his fingers gripping the back of his tie and collar in a vice.

He ignored the contamination of his pint as he knocked back a giant gulp and sparked up another Marlboro Light. He loosened his grip on Frank's collar and let him flop gently back to the floor behind the counter. Flynn reached across the counter. This time he placed his pint glass on the grill and pulled down the Guinness tap. The seductive black velvet flowed once again. Flynn allowed himself another chuckle and looked at his watch. The Funeral would be starting in less than half an hour. He toasted the lifeless body of Frank and poured the contents down his gullet. "Adios, Franco! Hope ye enjoyed the cherry! But don't worry, the best is yet to come!" Flynn brushed the speckles of blood into his black shirt. He could see movement outside, the funeral cortège was on its way…

Chapter Twenty-One: "You'll Never Walk Alone"

It was 6.30 am when the Gardaí had called to the door of the O'Reilly house. The squad car outside, a harbinger of doom. Anne collapsed in the hallway as Terry stood ghostly in the hallway, frozen in shock. Their only daughter, their own flesh and blood was dead. The Garda family liaison officer came into the house but her words fell on traumatised ears. Terry could see her lips moving but couldn't register any comprehension. Anne was bamboozled by a flatline noise which overcame her senses. This wrought hurt, a jack hammer into the nervous system. All bodily function cords had been severed inside their bodies. Anne began to involuntarily shake in convulsion, her eyes became distant and she fainted on the floor. They would have to identify the body. Phone their son in Australia. The early morning jogger who found Rachel had been taken to hospital with shock. Darkness descended on the Reilly family. A darkness that would envelop their souls and haunt them till their dying day.

The cortège snaked its way through Raheny village. It was Rachel's last journey. The ashen faced mourners followed. The community of Raheny, 'The Parish' as they called themselves, were close-knit and resolute. The tragedy of Rachel touched the hearts of everyone. Every conversation of the past forty-eight hours revolved around the horrific demise of Terry and Anne Reilly's daughter. The hearse passed the row of shops and navigated past the Watermill pub, the location where Terry had sat after his final interaction with his daughter. Through blurred, teary vision, he glanced across at the front door. The brass handled door. The same door he had pushed to enter on that fateful night before, commandeering his regular seat. The memory of his carefree stride as he entered that night came flooding back. He had confided in his best mate, Marto, that they were having a 'sticky' period at home with his daughter but that things had come to a head and he had "put her straight tonight." His bravado had embellished the recount of their family chat as a success. "Sometimes people just need to be told the way things are, straight down the line," as he gulped another long draft of his pint. "Ah you're fuckin' right man, fair play to ye for sorting that, great to hear she's back on the straight and narrow," replied Marto with discerning counsel. Neither could face the truth. Lies were much easier. Lies allowed them live in this parallel universe. A deflection from reality. God's waiting room, one by one they would drop dead and comfort themselves with tacky philosophies such as "live each day like it's your last." Liverpool had been playing a minor European cup match against a Spanish journeyman outfit Celta Vigo which ended in a one nil defeat in Anfield.

Terry recalls himself roaring belligerently at the big screen as the banter kicked off all around him, "sure that Gérard Houllier hasn't a fuckin' clue." A kaleidoscope of all the irrelevant nonsense on that night rumbled through his brain. Was he on his second or third pint when his daughter penned her suicide note? Was it the second half of the match when she went out walking? Was it the injury time chaos in the penalty box when he leapt from his seat and screamed for "a bleedin' peno" that she did the deed. When the fans echoed the Anfield anthem, 'You'll Never Walk Alone', was this the moment where she hung herself on the zip cord? All the fans together on the Kop with scarves around their neck. She was alone with a zip cord around her neck. Did she struggle? Did she cry out for help, but nobody came? Was she incapable of crying out for help? Did she try and save herself? Did she change her mind but just couldn't escape from the zip cord? Did she know she would die on her own? Did she suffer? A blackness washed over Terry as he began to lose consciousness. He knew he had to breathe. He gasped and recovered his breath slightly. Did someone make her do this to herself? Someone somewhere must have got inside her head. He tried to suck in the oxygen but it rebounded back off the roof of his trachea. *'Is everyone looking at me now because I'm the father who couldn't look after his own flesh and blood? The father who raised a daughter to hang herself.'* The questions catapulted around his head, each one landing a dagger inside his skull. He wheezed and tried vainly to suck in more air.

Recognising the heightened stress of his older brother, Wayne moved across and put a strong arm around his brother. Terry recoiled as he tried to loosen his tie. "I can't catch me breath, I can't fuckin' breathe." Wayne tried to usher him across to a nearby wall away from the cortège, "It's alright, brother, just sit here and try to get your breath." His black suit which he rented through the undertakers now seemed to be suffocating the life out of him. He opened the top buttons of his shirt and placed his head between his legs, frantically trying to control his heart rate and normalise his breathing. He was in the throes of a violent anxiety attack. He ran his fingers through his hair and clawed at his scalp with his fingernails. It was as if his body was under attack from itself. It was a shuddering internal assault of the senses. His dry and crusted scalp began to flake off as he continued mauling the top of his head. Perspiration drowned his body as the rented suit now stuck to him like an extra layer of skin. Dizziness swept over him as he tried to retain his balance and not fall backwards over the wall. He grabbed the sleeve of Wayne's suit to try anchor himself. Drowning man's grip. He thought about his own death. Who would really give a fuck if he passed from this world to the next? What sort of eulogy would they give, compliment him about driving the buses during the day and drinking pints at night in the Watermill? What good had he done on this planet? He vomited, the miniature yellow cobblestones from his mouth bounced on the pavement and splashed up his rented black shoes and trouser legs. His eyes watered furiously and fell like rain drops on his vomit. His hyperventilation and palpitations began to subside somewhat. The sweats began to crystallize on his skin. Internally, he felt repulsed that this violent attack couldn't take his pathetic life and put himself out of this misery.

A grey day rolled over Raheny, low and dense stratus clouds hovered above, seemingly within touching distance over the mourners heads, enhancing the state of suffocating grief. Anne was being held on either side by her two sisters as she ghosted along at the front of the cortège. Her sisters locked both her arms in an elbow link, akin to the orderlies transporting a recently tranquillised inpatient in the nuthouse. She had been sedated twice in the last forty-eight hours and still displayed a far away look in her eyes. Shock had paralysed her grief from the moment she collapsed in her porch, when the numbness wore off and the trauma took over they had to call a doctor for her. She hadn't eaten and had hardly spoken since the event. She had been given a cocktail of 'benzos' that morning designed to curb a breakdown whilst keeping her semi lucid. The dosage was overcautious and overcooked as she was now a dribbling mess, unable to control the salivating from her mouth and her nostrils now ran freely.

Both sisters assiduously wiped her nose and mouth with handkerchiefs as they tried to inconspicuously stem the flow. It added an extra layer of ignominy to the nightmare. A doctor had also been chartered to be on hand during the funeral in the event that the earlier medicinal cocktail wasn't potent enough to see her through the day. Anne may have seemed comatose to the outside world but she was very much alive inside. The equivalent of locked-in-syndrome, fully aware of the outside world but incapable of interaction. She wholeheartedly felt every ounce of the mourners' sympathy but her only physical acknowledgement amounted to the tears and mucus which cascaded down her face. Repulsive fury. The humiliation of being drugged at her own daughter's funeral. A tempest bubbled inside her. Her shell-shocked eyes belied the cognitive function within. She had been married to a narcissistic pig for a quarter of a century, her only daughter temporarily resided in a pine box, in the back of a black limousine and would soon permanently reside in the cemetery forever more. Her own life had been a purgatory of mediocrity at best, her softness had led to her being bullied.

She felt skeletal, as if her insides had been ripped apart with razor blades. Her mother used to work in Harry's Fishmongers on Capel street. Bizarrely, her mind filtered back to the time as a child when she would hang around the shop waiting for her mother to finish up work. She remembered the sawdust and blood drenched floor. She used to be traumatised as the workers nonchalantly chopped off the fish heads and tails, leaving only the torso exposed on the chopping block. They even chatted and told jokes whilst committing this barbaric slaughter. They would then use the long filleting knife for disembowelment, severing a long ravine with surgical precision before flattening out the body for the final act, the removal of the fish spine. She recalled the clinical efficiency of the blade as it seamlessly separated the bone structure from the fillet. The fish were then placed on the steep shelf of ice for sale. The place made her nauseous. She used to think about those fish and what waters they swam in. Were they happy before they were caught? Did their mother try to save them? What age were they? Did they know they were going to end up in a fish shop on Capel Street? Did they suffer or was it painless? She remembered crying about the fish at nighttime. Lying in her bed with tears streaming down her face. Her father always laughed it off, "Haven't you little to be worrying about," he would say, always after a night's drinking. Her mother was a gentle soul. She knew that working at Harry's fish shop was a horror show and the pay was terrible but it was the only work she could find. She needed the money to support the family. Anne could never remember being happy, really happy. She used to love playing on her own with her dolls and teddies, where she could recreate a happy family and a happy world for herself. At night, she used to hold her bunny 'Simon' close to her as she closed her eyes and went to sleep. Always dreaming of a better life, always dreaming of easier and happier times. Those times never came. All she had was her dreams. And now this. She felt the strong grip of her sisters on either side as she looked ahead at the hearse. She thought of all the dreams she had with her bunny 'Simon'. She would marry a prince and become a beautiful Princess. They would live in a castle and live happily ever after. Her nose began to run again as her sister dabbed it gently with a tissue.

Terry began to gather himself and rejoined the peloton of mourners. He rose unsteadily on his feet and wiped the vomit from his mouth. An ignominious spectacle with so many eyes trained on him. Some of the gathering surmised that he was most probably on the drink and this meltdown the result of over intoxication. Such assumptions could only be garnered over years of being a piss head. The locals of Raheny knew him well, steady enough sort of fella, you'd trust him to a drive a bus but little else. Typical 'ham and egg' working class soldier. Splattered vomit still adorned the bottom of his trouser legs, he leant forward to try brush clean the solids but only succeeded in wiping the sick from his hands back onto his trousers. Wayne handed him a tissue. He accepted it and put it in his pocket. He would carry on as he was, nothing was going to change anybody's opinion of him. Going to church smelling like vomit for his daughter's funeral. Nothing mattered any more. He paused for a moment and looked skywards as the dark clouds sunk lower. What good had he done in this life? Trading places and sliding doors. He should be the one dangling from the zipline. What loss would he have been? One less drunk shouting at the big screen down in the Watermill. The violent grief burned the walls of his stomach and made their way up his oesophagus and into his throat as his eyes began to well up. His head haemorrhaged in pain as the trauma crystallised into tears. Wayne ushered him back towards the top of the cortège where he returned to his station beside the family. He looked at his wife in her quasi-comatose state, snot dripping down her face as her sisters tried in vain to soak up the discharge. What would the future hold now? A life with this dribbling maniac?

He never gave her proper love and treated her like shite. And now the chickens, hens and cockerels would come home to roost. No doubt she would be heavily tranquillised before undergoing extensive treatment for post-traumatic stress, depression, anxiety, mental disorder and every other diagnosis the medical glitterati dreamt up to maintain their compliant files. The psych doctors would have a field day experimenting with dosage whilst the pharmaceutical companies would have another test pig for their latest inventions. All the while he would have to endure her breakdowns, mood swings, forgetfulness and frenzied anxiety attacks.

In a few days, his son would fly back to Australia. He was already estranged from the family and it was touch and go whether he would even come back for the funeral. Once the formality of his departure was confirmed, they would be properly on their own. The very thought of being shoehorned into a supportive relationship as a husband asphyxiated his senses. He didn't love her any more. He hadn't loved her for a long time. She knew it too and just accepted it for what it was. She was soft and he took advantage of her. A doormat.

Terry looked at Anne cradled between her sisters at the front of the cortège. He visualised his escape hatch. He could pack his bags and elope to Shamrock Terrace, a bit of a dump but could probably get used to it. A life with Grace. She was damaged goods and emotionally unhinged but still a better bet than arriving home to face Anne every night with the four walls suffocating the life out of him. Perhaps he would make good on his promises to Grace after all. All of these narcissistic thoughts flooded his brain, his conscious mind tried to focus on the grief at hand. The hearse carrying his deceased daughter only yards away and yet plans for self-preservation dominated his thoughts.

Perhaps we would go on living a double life. He could also justify spending even more time in the Watermill as part of 'the grieving process.' He wouldn't tell Grace about his daughter's death. What good would that do? Open up an emotional can of worms about tragic bereavement, unite them in grief? Shamrock Terrace was a halfway house to get his end away and kill a few hours. Last thing he wanted was for it to morph into some fucked up counselling session. He resolved himself that the double life was the way to go. Much less hassle. If things got out of hand at home he could review the situation but he didn't plan on being there much anyway.

Going forward he would make sure that Anne would be in bed by the time he got home. He would be numbed with the drink, so even if she kicked off it would fall on deaf ears. Between overtime, normal working hours, Shamrock Terrace and the Watermill he would fill his days. He would continue to fill Grace with empty promises. What choice would she have anyway? She wasn't exactly inundated with offers. No doubt some day he would drop dead but now wasn't the time to face up to anything. He would never change, if anything he would get worse and worse. They would finally have to cart his rotten carcass off to the boneyard but that would be their problem, his burial arrangements were of no concern to him. He would be worm feed and quickly forgotten.

Flynn

Chapter Twenty-Two: The Homecoming

A crucible of suffering awaited the mourners as they packed into the church. A tortured soul had been released into the afterlife. This was now the penultimate destination for Rachel's body before the final farewell of the crematorium. The great irony of death. For someone who felt so alone all her life, she was now surrounded by heartbroken sympathisers. But it was too late, there was no going back. She had expedited the crossing of the bridge between life and death by her own hand. She wanted for a better place and rolled the dice. Nobody in attendance could say exactly whether she found it or not but the passing of a young girl had paralysed the community. The suffocating silence was finally punctured by alter bells beckoning the congregation to rise. The synchronised liberation of the church pews. Each mourner endeavoured not to make a sound, yet collectively, the air was pierced by a few seconds of subtle rustling before the deathly silence descended once again. The priest departed the sacristy and slowly and methodically made his way towards the pulpit. Head bowed in unity with the mourners. He spoke eloquently and with kind compassion. To all those present, he was a conduit for spirituality. Carrying out his chosen vocation in life. To all except one. A pair of shark eyes beamed from the back of the church. The eyes of a dead man… or perhaps those of a dead child. Flynn's mouth went dry. His eyes began to water. "We meet again," he whispered in an inaudible tone. He tried to take a deep breath but only stimulated a feral grunting from the back of his throat. He gnashed his teeth together and exposed his canines…"We meet again…" Saliva drooped over his bottom lip and trickled down his chin. His dead eyes remained transfixed on the ceremonial chief in the ostentatious robes. "Custard cream eating fuck," he muttered. "I think it's time me and you had a chat…"

The church service embodied the excruciating grief of a family in ruins. Ghosts from Rachel's past stood with their heads bowed. Old school friends and acquaintances who had lost touch. Many of whom felt riddled with guilt that they hadn't reached out more often. Perhaps earlier intervention would have arrested the slide into the abyss. A simple call or a coffee and a chat, who knows, it might have changed the course of history but there was no going back now. "See you all on the other side," her suicide note had read. She had harboured no ill will towards anyone. Yet the feeling of isolation and failure had defined her life. A crushing poem read by Rachel's brother brought the curtain down on the formalities;

I was at the edge of a cliff,
Ready to jump,
I looked to you,
Hoping you'd try to stop me.
You looked at me
And sighed
Because you were tired
Of trying to help me.
By the time you took
A single step forward,
I was already
Plummeting towards
The ground.

Flynn

His voice wavered as grief stretched the skin around his cheekbones. His jaw fought desperately to hold back a tsunami of tears. All in vain, he succumbed to human nature as the piercing grief drowned his senses. He slumped down from the altar. A broken man. The choice of poem was a broadside at those who gave up on Rachel, none more so than himself. An older brother living aloof in Australia. What had he ever done for Rachel? He, too, had blood on his hands. There was no applause. The congregation recoiled from the harrowing undertones.

The priest wore a look of disdain towards such rhetoric. It wasn't the words of consolation that perhaps he was expecting. He waited several moments before closing out the mass. The lighting of incense and the words he had reiterated thousands of times; "Eternal rest grant unto them, O Lord, and let perpetual light shine upon them. May their souls and the souls of all the faithful departed, through the mercy of God, rest in peace. Amen"

A wry smile shot across Flynn's face as he heard those final words of solace. "And he believes every word of it," he hissed. The pallbearers encircled Rachel's coffin. The first steps of her final journey commenced. The church began to slowly empty out. A few whispers became audible as a gentle thaw came over the gathering. The powerful scent of incense hung in the air. Soon only Flynn remained. He lit up two candles. "They both have it coming," he uttered with a wry smile. He blessed himself in mock reverence and refocused his glare back on the altar. The priest and the altar boys had long disappeared back to the sacristy.

Flynn

"Time to get reacquainted."

Flynn paused at the foot of the altar for symbolic genuflection. He looked at the pulpit and the grand designs in homage of God. *Judgement day has arrived.* He traversed through the back of the altar and into the sacristy. The interior hadn't changed much. The same route he had navigated in the darkest days of his childhood. A stairwell faced him which led to the private vestry of the priest. His heart jolted as the violent memories hijacked his thoughts. Furious anger reverberated deep inside his gut. He felt nauseated. A familiar aroma filled his lungs, the unique, piercing scent from Major cigarettes. The atmospheric surrounds were threatening to reignite the trauma all over again. The beast inside began to growl. He had come for vengeance, this was no time to let emotions subvert his objective. He placed a foot on the first step, a familiar creaking noise perforated the silence. The sound that acted as a harbinger of doom many years ago. The same sound echoed through his head the first day he was invited back to the private room. The sound and the fury. Today he would bring his own fury. The scent got even more potent the closer he got to the door. He felt a presence within. A familiar voice barked, "Hello? Who's there? Is that you, Brendan?" Flynn pushed the door open. "Ah hello, Father, sorry for the intrusion… I enjoyed the service so much that I felt compelled to come back here and tell you in person."

The priest was at his old mahogany desk, an ashtray smouldered beside him, overflowing with cigarette stubs. There was also a smell of drink, hard liquor, yet no bottle was visible.

He turned to make eye contact with the intruder. "Well I appreciate the gesture but you shouldn't be up here. This is a private chamber and I'm afraid you'll have to leave." Flynn tilted his head to the left as if to recalibrate what was just said. He flashed a glance at the table beside him, a box of Major cigarettes stared back at him, just as they had many years ago.

"No problem, Father, hope you don't mind if I help myself to one of these before I go?" Flynn pointed to the open box of Majors. The priest was growing impatient with each passing moment, "In fact I'd rather you just left now," he paused and exhaled with growing irritation, "however, if you must then please help yourself to a cigarette but you must leave immediately." Flynn smiled back at him, "Muchas gracias, Padre," he leaned across and took a cigarette from the box and slowly placed it in his mouth. He turned to leave before pausing theatrically at the door, "Sorry, Father, I almost forgot, could I trouble you for a light?" This latest procrastination was met with even greater vexation, the Priest hauled himself back to his feet and grabbed the lighter from the table. He sparked the flint wheel and held it aloft for Flynn, "Now please leave immediately, you must leave right NOW!" his voice echoed out in the corridor.

Flynn gently sucked down on the perfectly combusted flax paper. He inhaled slowly and smiled. "Mmm, now that's a strong cigarette, Father. Ooooh!" Flynn's jawline contorted as he recoiled from the powerful nicotine detonation in his lungs. "You'll be meeting God sooner than you think if you keep smoking them," he beamed him his smile.

"Okay, now that's enough, just please leave." The Priest placed a hand on his shoulder to usher him out the door. Flynn stopped dead in his tracks and shot a daggering glare towards the hand on his shoulder blade. "Why, Father, it's been a while since you've laid your hands of God on these shoulders..." He took a deep meaningful drag and engaged eye contact. The Priest stared right back at him, a steely gaze. Unwavering and unrepentant. "Well, Father..." he paused momentarily, "Ye know it's just occurred to me that I'm calling you Father and I don't even know your fuckin' name. My own Father is dead... And yet I'm calling you *Father*!" Flynn barked a loud laugh. "Life is truly ironic," Flynn took a giant drag of his cigarette and grimaced, "how the fuck do you smoke them, Father?" He chuckled a bellowing guttural laugh.

Silence.

Eye contact was maintained. A Mexican stand-off in the vestry. Flynn broke the silence, "Daryl... Daryl Flynn..." He uttered his second name with heightened intonation. The Priest's pupils became dilated. He retreated backwards across the room. A scent of vengeance pierced the air. He slowly collapsed back in his chair. With trembling hands he pawed across the table and procured another Major. He managed to spark up a light and inhaled deeply. Feigning composure he looked again in Flynn's direction, he nonchalantly flicked some ash into the ashtray beside him, "And how have you been... Daryl? Flynn flashed him a smile. "Well it's been all plain sailing, Father, you taught me great life lessons during my time here. Particularly in this very room."

Flynn paused and looked around, "I don't suppose you have any more Custard Creams lying around for my way home?" He boomed a giant laugh which reverberated around the whole sacristy. "So I've been busy out there, Father… Out there in the world, finding myself. And now I'm a Trinity Boy! Not bad for a bastard child with a promiscuous mother… Growing up in a council house… All the reasons why you recruited me all those years ago." Flynn took a deep breath and sighed, "The weak preyed on the weaker…"

He looked down at the spot where his virgin rape had occurred. The speckle of blood he had transfixed on all those years ago. "But what happens when the weak get stronger, Father? And they come back…"
The priest held his gaze. A cornered rat. "Well, Daryl, I'm delighted to see you and it sounds as if you're doing well but I'm under great pressure to attend to my parishioners. Now, if you'll excuse me, I've work to do."
Flynn inhaled another drag of his Major, "Father… the moment for judgement is fast approaching. In fact, I think the moment of judgement could well be upon us." A psychotic smile illuminated his face. He pulled down a roped cincture from a hook on the wall, the same cincture which the Priest had worn during the funeral service. "I hope you believe in fate, a beautiful end to a beautiful life. I'm sure you've pondered this question for years… sitting up there in the parish house… all the years spent in the seminary. Well, here I am, Father… It's me… Fate! In a few moments, you're going to die. Perhaps you'll meet God… perhaps you won't. If I was a betting man, I'd say Beelzebub is fixing your bedsheets as we speak." He exhaled another plume of smoke in the priest's direction and followed it up with another psychotic grin. He threw the cigarette butt on

the wooden floor and stubbed it out with his foot. With both hands now free, he wrapped the cincture around his knuckles and formed a perfect arc for strangulation. He jolted the cincture twice and smiled, content in the knowledge that the rope cord could withstand the force of what was to come.

Flynn walked slowly and methodically towards his prey. "You'll have to excuse the summary justice being administered here today but I'm sure you'll agree that you're guilty as hell… any last words, Father?"

There was silence.

The Priest looked him in the eyes and trembled, "Hell awaits us both, Daryl!" He covertly cupped the ashtray with his right hand. Flynn barrelled a giant laugh. "Well, be sure and send me a postcard, Father." Flynn stood his full height over him. "You had this coming…"

Suddenly, a feral roar pierced the air as the ashtray smashed against Flynn's temple. The ivory ashtray shattered upon impact. A deep gash opened up below Flynn's hairline and claret trickled down his cheek. Flynn jolted backwards. A slightly dazed feeling came over him, but he immediately returned eye contact. He allowed the cincture cord to loosen and raised his right hand to assess the damage. He dabbed his brow and procured a large ravine of blood which ran through his palm. "Nice…" He whispered as the smile returned to his face. "First blood to you, Father." The Priest stood trembling in shock as to how this hadn't incapacitated his assailant. He swallowed deeply and began hyperventilating. "So you do believe in

God after all." Flynn barked out a chuckle. He clenched his bloodied right hand and flushed a jab straight into his jaw. The Priest tumbled back onto the chair. He cowered in terror as the force of the punch and impending doom became a reality. His resistance was over.

"Please… Please…" He begged and raised his trembling hands in the air. A submissive plea for mercy. Flynn rocked his head backwards in reverberating laughter, "Judgement day is upon us, Father!" His attention was briefly stolen by a drop of blood that had now made landfall on the wooden floor. The speckle reignited a rage inside his cranium as the dark thoughts of abuse flooded his mind. He gnashed his teeth together, crunching down hard on the enamel.

"Just like the old days, Father… Think of this as your final absolution for all the ghosts of the past."

He reformed his bond with the cincture cord and arced it into a loop. "Please… No! Please!" bellowed the priest in a high-pitched scream. Flynn jammed the cincture cord over the priest's head and pulled it tightly at the front. The perfect noose was now set for execution. "Look into my eyes… Look into my fuckin' eyes, you rapist fuck!" roared Flynn, his voice reverberating around the vestry. He could feel the breath of the priest again. That breath of cigarettes and alcohol. The same breath he was now about to take away. Flynn began to pull the cords together. The priest clawed frantically, his nails breaking the skin on Flynn's face. Flynn tightened the cord as the Priest's body began to convulse in involuntary spasm. His eyeballs doubled in size and spittle ejected from his mouth.

He engaged Flynn in one last wide-eyed contact, "You can burn in hell, Daryl Flynn!"

The blood vessels protruded on his neck as he fought for his final breath. "I think it's only right we say one last prayer together, Father… For old time's sake." Flynn could feel the life draining out of the Priest. Their time together was coming to an end.

"May God Almighty have mercy on us,
Forgive us our sins,
And bring us to everlasting life.
Amen."

The priest's eyes went dead just as Flynn said the word Amen. A gentle wheeze gave way as his windpipe collapsed. Flynn's knuckles oozed blood from the chaffing of the cincture rope. He maintained his bind for several more seconds before allowing the priest to slide slowly onto the floor, beside the spot where it all began.

Flynn picked up another Major cigarette from the box and reclined back in the chair. He exhaled loudly as he relinquished his grip from the cord. He ceremoniously raised it above his head and allowed it to fall on top of the vanquished. He sparked up and placed his feet up on the table. The vestry was deathly quiet. No sign of the cavalry. He had time.

He noticed a bottle of Napoleon brandy stashed under the mahogany desktop. "Don't mind if I do…" He grabbed a teacup from the table and threw out its contents. He poured out a large measure and looked down at the lifeless body on the floor. He took a long gulp of brandy and smiled.

"Happy trails, Father," he toasted the cadaver.

"Still one candle left…"

Acknowledgements

To those who believe in the exploration of self and the continued search for answers, I salute you.

To those who have yet to explore the darker inner workings of their human spirit, I wish you well. Don't leave it too long as life is short...

To Mairtin Breathnach and all his team at Universal Media - your positivity and brilliance paved the way to bring this project to life. To the genius of Stephanie Leone and Jack Mullen, I hope this is only the start of a beautiful and psychotic journey together.

To all those who have put up with my madness and volatility over the years, I offer you my sincere thanks.

www.ingramcontent.com/pod-product-compliance
Lightning Source LLC
Chambersburg PA
CBHW020333310726
48979CB00015B/2348/J

* 9 7 8 1 7 3 9 9 7 4 2 0 6 *